Ellie Dwyer's Great Escape

Diane Winger

Copyright © 2019 Diane Winger

All rights reserved.

This is a work of fiction. Names, characters, organizations, places, events, and incidents are either products of the author's imagination or are used fictitiously.

No part of this book may be reproduced, or stored in a retrieval system, or transmitted in any form or by any means, electronic, mechanical, photocopying, recording, or otherwise, without express written permission of the author.

ISBN-13: 978-1796750164

DEDICATION

To my amazing husband:
May you remain forever enthusiastic, forever entertaining, and forever young.

ACKNOWLEDGMENTS

Once again, my friend and talented editor, Val Burnell, has brought her keen eye and language skills to help make this story shine. Talented Christine Savoie created another wonderful cover. Many thanks to both of them.

As always, my husband, Charlie (not to be confused with Charli the cat), has been my rock. His unlimited energy, enthusiasm for adventure, and ability to make me laugh always inspire me to move beyond my self-imposed limits and reach for the sky. I can't wait for our next outing in our "Wingmobile" – our wonderful little Aliner camper.

I'd also like to acknowledge all my fellow campers who've shared their stories with me in various social media groups. Thanks especially to Gregory Dault, Linda Cannizzaro, and Jim Scott for your tales of falling camper walls, hotdog-stealing seagulls, and entertained audiences watching you set up and put down your A-frame camper.

Finally, my sincere thanks to everyone who has taken the time to read my novels. I hope you've found them interesting, entertaining, and perhaps even a bit inspiring. I welcome your feedback on my work, as I learn more about the craft of writing from each comment.

Chapter 1

If bad luck really does come in threes, I've finally reached my quota.

All in all, this feels like the least calamitous of the three, although I doubt the rest of the people hunkered down on their cots in this musty church basement would agree. We were among the early wave of evacuees. The young woman on my right is a self-appointed "breaking news" anchor, her focus seldom wavering from her smart phone as she announces how many people are now housed in the covered stadium that's supposedly far enough from the coast to avoid the worst of the winds and the expected storm surge. The larger the population at the stadium grows, the more relieved I am at being among this smaller crowd of around fifty, despite the cramped quarters.

First thing tomorrow, I plan to hit the road again to try to make it to my brother-in-law's. I guess I can still call him that – Franklin and I aren't actually divorced, and Hank's been nearly as baffled and pissed off by his brother's Disappearing Act – as we've come to call it – as I've been. It's kind of Hank and Cheryl to invite me to wait out the storm at their place, especially not knowing if my own apartment will be habitable once this passes. I've already decided I won't be returning, even if it survives the wrath of Hurricane Janelle. There's no longer anything for me there.

"The stadium's housing up to 20,000 people now and all the lanes on the interstate have been changed to westbound only," my neighbor announces to anyone listening. She sets her phone down for a moment as she pulls her hair loose from its elastic band, shakes it out, finger-combs it, then ties it all back up in what looks to me like the exact same messy bun she had before. Farther down our row of cots, a baby is screaming as its mother tries to help a little boy clean bubble gum off his face with one hand while cradling the crying infant against her other shoulder. I consider going over to offer some help, but my total lack of experience with small children convinces me to stay put.

A woman dims the overhead lights. Like all the volunteers, she's clad in a bright green t-shirt adorned with the word "Coexist," spelled out using religious symbols. Other green-shirted helpers set small battery-powered lanterns at intervals along the bookcases lining the walls. I scan the room. Some parents have succeeded in getting their kids to lie down, but others seem to have given up, their thousand-mile stares as evidence that they are no longer registering the shrieks and shouts of children racing around the perimeter of the large room, banging into people unlucky enough to be near their paths. An older woman like myself grabs a boy of about ten by the arm and scolds him after he nearly bowls her over. She releases him and stretches her arms toward the ceiling, then lowers herself uncomfortably onto her cot. My back is starting to ache from trying to sit without support, so I sprawl onto my back and stuff my sweater under my knees for relief.

A feeling of despair seems to permeate the room, but I'm just plain tired. This is nothing compared to our exodus two years ago and 2,500 miles from here. Most people have never been driven from their homes by a natural disaster. Why is it my fate to endure such a trauma twice? Why the hell do I have to do this alone this time? Where is Franklin?

The hours flow past at a glacial pace. Eventually, the space grows relatively silent, the only sounds being an unsyncopated pattern of snores and deep breathing, interspersed with the occasional moan or incoherent mumble. I doze, but can't resist checking my watch, disappointed to realize that it's only been twelve minutes since I last looked.

I must have fallen asleep again. I awaken with a start from a dream of loading our car. Yes, our car, not just mine. Franklin was there – as he was in real life – carrying the boxes and bags of clothing and photo albums while I stuffed in my laptop and jewelry box and the contents from our fire box. We raced to drive away from our California home through dense smoke, just like what actually happened. But then my dream veered off its usual course. Franklin was still at the wheel as I somehow stood upright on the passenger seat and spotted a wall of water thundering down the canyon behind us, threatening to wash us away. The smoke and fires were gone, but we were about to drown instead.

My wildfire nightmares are nothing new, but I'm dismayed to have this latest natural disaster start to invade my dreams as well. Wasn't one enough?

I hope my stuff is safe inside my locked vehicle. They said there'd be a volunteer watching the church parking lot all night to make sure nobody breaks a window or jimmies a lock. I tossed a blanket over the boxes in the back, but maybe that would just make a thief even more sure that there's something of value worth snatching.

Having been through something like this before, I feel like an expert. I may not have been one of the very first to pack up and head inland, but I wasn't going to play that wait and see game again. I packed everything I cared about keeping – which wasn't all that much – and left well before the storm was expected to reach land.

I'd hate to have my things stolen. I've already left so much behind.

Moving as quietly as I can, I slip into my shoes and neatly fold the blanket at the foot of the cot. Fetching my tote bag from underneath the make-shift bed, I tiptoe past my sleeping neighbors and return a polite wave from a middle-aged woman lying with her hands tucked behind her head. Before I can react, my tote bumps against a card table laden with large, overflowing bowls of apples and oranges. A cascade of fruit tumbles noisily to the floor and fruit rolls in all directions. I drop to my knees and try to corral a stampede of oranges with both arms before they can spread too far. Someone snickers, a child whimpers, and a couple of sympathetic souls join me in rounding up the wayward fruit.

"I'm so sorry!" I whisper to those nearby as I separate the fallen apples from the oranges. "I'll go wash these."

A pair of church volunteers wearing their signature Coexist shirts have arrived. "Don't worry about it," the woman whispers in my ear. "We'll take care of everything. You go ahead – we've got this covered."

Her partner helps me to my feet. "Will you be staying with us again tonight?" he asks.

I shake my head. "No, I'm driving on to my in-laws' place. I'd hoped to make it there yesterday, but the traffic was so heavy and slow I decided I needed to take a break. Thanks to all you folks for doing this." I clutch my tote bag tightly to my chest to avoid any further mishaps and make my way up the stairs.

"Can't sleep?" a man asks as I approach my SUV in the dim light of very early morning. I'm startled at first, but spot the familiar green shirt and relax.

"Not really." My Jeep Cherokee unlocks with a series of beeps as I click the remote.

"How about some hot coffee for the road?"

I mumble a weak protest about his going to the trouble, but he's already jogging over to a gazebo to fetch a cup. As he returns, the delicious aroma hits me from thirty feet away, and I start salivating in anticipation.

"Thank you so much."

"No problem. Will you be back for tonight?"

"No. I'll be staying with family," I say as I accept the coffee and climb into my vehicle, anxious to be on my way.

Family. What I wouldn't give to have my parents still around. Much as I love my brother-in-law, it's just not the same as being comforted by Mom or Dad when I'm feeling down. My throat tightens and I feel on the verge of tears. I take a few bracing swallows of the coffee and straighten my back, determined to regain control of myself. Then I'm on my way, aiming toward Hank and Cheryl's place. What my plans are after that is anyone's guess.

Chapter 2

"But where will you *go*?"

You'd think I had just revealed that I was planning on taking a one-way spaceship to Mars, the way my sister-in-law asks the question, all googly-eyed, her mouth hanging open, shocked at my revelation of my plans. Or lack thereof.

"I haven't decided yet. Somewhere out west, but not as far as California. Been there, burned that." I know I sound flip, but Cheryl sometimes brings that out in me. Maybe a counterpoint to her being such a drama queen about everything.

"Have you thought about returning to Denver?" Hank asks.

The idea of returning to my childhood stomping grounds is actually somewhat depressing. I'll bet the population has quadrupled or more since I graduated high school many decades ago. "Too big and housing is too expensive. Although I'm not ruling out other parts of Colorado. I suppose I'll know where I want to land when I get there. Wherever 'there' is."

This gets a rise out of Cheryl. "But where will you stay? It's really not safe for a woman traveling by herself – especially older women like us! You need to make arrangements in advance, not just show up in a city and hope you can find a safe neighborhood to stay in."

"Listen, I'll figure it out. I appreciate your concern, but if I can make it through being chased from our home by a wildfire, I'm sure I can handle this." I force a light and confident tone to my voice, but the truth is that she's honed in on the same worries that jockey for attention in my brain as I've tried to sleep these past few nights.

Then she drops the bomb. "But you had Franklin with you back then."

Yes, I did. Thanks so much for pointing that out. "I'll manage." God, I need to gather my courage and head out of here soon.

Hank rises from his lawn chair and stretches tall, grunting and creaking as he unfolds to his full height. He runs his fingers through his still-thick mane of steel gray hair. Franklin has also avoided signs of balding, but at age 66, he sports a lush head of white hair rather than gray. Hank's mannerisms and vocalizations are so similar to my husband's that I feel a momentary catch in my throat. "I need to walk," he declares, squinting at the setting sun. "Who wants to join me?"

As expected, Cheryl declines and I accept. I've just been rescued from his wife's interrogation – a temporary reprieve.

We stroll in silence for almost two blocks before Hank speaks. "No word from Frankie, I gather."

Franklin hates being called that. Hank only does it when he's giving his kid brother a hard time.

"Still nothing." I thrust my hands deep into the pockets of my capris and try breathing deeply, staving off the anger and disappointment that have certainly waned over the past eight-plus months, but are always lurking beneath the surface. A part of me had been dreaming that Franklin had reached out to Hank since we last checked in with each other. I've got to stop nursing these tiny sparks of hope. I keep burning myself with them.

"That idiot. You'd think he could at least send you an email and make sure you got out okay. Even if he really has turned into a hermit and is living in a cave, you'd think he'd have heard about the hurricane and evacuations."

When my husband walked out on me, spouting some nonsense about "I need space" and "it's not you, it's me" – phrases he must have resurrected from our pseudo-hippie college days – I was too astonished at first to believe he was actually leaving. Even when he didn't return the next day, or the day after that, I was certain he'd be back any moment. I cried, I slammed his pillow onto the bed until I couldn't raise my arms again, I sat and stared out the window watching for him to pull into the driveway, I screamed, I ate cookies by the boxful. I questioned myself, racked my brain for clues as to why he would do such a thing. I told no one. Hell, I barely connected with anyone for weeks. Hank was the first person I finally reached out to.

I wouldn't describe the brothers' relationship as especially close, but it wasn't distant by any means either. They could go a month or longer without talking on the phone, but they always seemed to connect whenever they did have news to share or just wanted to catch up. We only got together in person two or maybe three times per year, even though Franklin made such a big deal about moving back to the east coast after we fled California so he could be closer to "family" – meaning Hank, who doesn't even live on the coast any more. But Franklin seemed to need to return to his roots, and he had recently retired so we could live just about anywhere. So we moved to a place that was a day's drive from his brother, but felt like home to Franklin. To me? Not so much.

Hank was as shocked as I was when I told him his brother had walked out. He's always been easy to talk to – I felt like we were old friends within five minutes of meeting him for the first time when Franklin and I were first starting to get serious. He's never wavered in his support of me since his brother left. He's tried calling, emailing, texting, and messaging on social media, thinking Franklin was ignoring my efforts, but might respond to his brother. We've concluded that my husband really has canceled his old phone number, deactivated or deleted his email and other accounts, and seemingly dropped out of our universe. His Disappearing Act.

"So, Ellie, how are you fixed for money? You know you can count on me if you need a little help during this transition."

Interesting that he said "me" and not "us."

"Yes, well, thanks for asking. But I'm good. Really. Don't worry about that. Your brother wasn't a complete jerk, at least not in that respect." I don't go into detail, but Franklin quietly withdrew precisely half of the balances of both our checking and savings accounts, down to the penny, and made the next six months' rent payments in advance – from his "half," as best I could determine. His Social Security deposit didn't show up three weeks later, however, so I assume he switched that to a new account he opened just in his own name. The automatic payments for utilities are still being taken out of my account, but the car payments for our newer sedan – the one he took without asking me which vehicle I wanted to keep – haven't been withdrawn since he left.

He arranged it all like a judge putting together a fair split of assets in a divorce. Only there was never any mention of divorce, and so far I haven't had the additional slap in the face of being served with papers. I vacillate between thinking that's a good thing or bad.

We continue our walk in silence. The sun has dipped below the horizon, but the temperature is barely easing. My blouse clings to my back, but the sweat doesn't evaporate to cool me, not like it would in so many arid places out west. I miss Colorado. Even California, back before the fires destroyed the beautiful, tree-filled slopes of the mountains surrounding our lovely home. I remember the cool breezes in the evenings as we sat out on our deck and gazed at the peaks and the blaze of reds and oranges in the sky as the light began to fade. We thought we were so safe, with our "defensible space" around our stone-façade home. It survived the fire, but we hadn't realized how much damage the smoke could cause. And our views – our beloved views! Blackened.

"I'm ready to turn around," I say, wiping my forehead with the back of my hand.

We reverse course.

"I have a question for you," Hank says, his too casual tone sounding like he's been rehearsing this question in his head. "Have you considered finding a place around here? I mean, Cheryl and the kids and I are the only family you have any more, right? We'd love to have you closer by, share Thanksgiving, Christmas, birthdays – things like that."

Hank is a sweetheart, but we both know that Cheryl would be lukewarm at best with seeing more of me. And their "kids" – both in their forties now – are pretty much strangers to me as adults. I can't even remember where Robert and his wife are living now – Connecticut, maybe? Lana's in Michigan and has a new boyfriend. If it weren't for Facebook, I wouldn't be able to recognize either of them, nor their children.

I thank my brother-in-law for his kind suggestion, but insist that I want to settle far west of the Mississippi.

"Fair enough," he says, "but let's not lose touch, okay? I still consider you to be my little sister."

Blinking back tears, I throw my arms around him and hug him tightly. He pats my back as he probably did to his daughter when she was a girl who needed a supportive hug from her daddy. "Love you, Hank," I manage to mumble.

"Love you too, Ellie."

Chapter 3

Back when we used to go on road trips, Franklin and I would often drive for nine or ten hours, trading off behind the wheel and making only a few pit stops for fuel, food, and bathroom breaks. I managed seven hours of actual driving yesterday, but today I'm giving up even sooner. I've got it in my head that I want to be up in the mountains of good old Colorado, where I can escape this heat and dust and the stink of enormous dairy farms, with the dominant scenery being the next town's silo or water tower. Somebody can tell Dorothy that we've located Kansas.

I pull into a larger town and use my phone to search for an area with hotels. After a rude awakening yesterday at the cost of lodging, I select one of the lower-priced facilities with online reviews that make it sound adequate for one night. Clean bed and bathroom, hot shower – what more do I need?

Okay, so maybe I should add to my criteria a bed that doesn't sag like an ancient horse's back and towels that aren't so thin I can see through them. But it's only one night and I think back on all those people still back in the church basement or crowded into a football stadium and count myself blessed.

I've lugged to the room my laptop and a small duffel with a change of clothes for the morning, plus my toiletries. Thinking I'll try to get some work done this evening, I've also brought up a box with my reference books and the briefcase where I've stashed all the important papers that we used to keep in the fire box. Insurance, car title for the Jeep, marriage license (for what that's worth), and the like.

Once I set up a work area on the wobbly round table in my room, instead of opening up the manuscript I've been proofreading, I pull up the spreadsheet I created while staying at Hank and Cheryl's, hoping the numbers will have magically grown larger in the income column and smaller in the expense column. Instead, I force myself to increase the value beside "lodging" and I feel my headache from all that time in the car intensify to make the back of my head throb.

Massaging my neck with one hand, I speak out loud, a habit I seem to have developed since Hank walked out. "Okay, Ellie, you can apply for Social Security now instead of waiting till age sixty-six like you planned." Yes, I call myself by name when I give myself a pep talk. I already know what benefit I can draw, so I plug in that number. I reduce what I've estimated for lodging starting next month, hoping I'll figure out a landing spot and find an inexpensive place to rent by then. There'll probably be some insurance money coming my way, but that will only provide a brief reprieve before I need to balance my budget.

Of course, there's my IRA. In all the planning Franklin and I have done in the past, we weren't going to touch my account until I turned seventy. We figured we could stretch those funds out for twenty years or so, when combined with what he still had in his retirement plan. I'll have to rework all those numbers.

I could live out of my SUV for a while. Sort of. I'd have to figure out where to stash about a third of my boxes and bags to clear enough space so I could lie down in the back. Memories of one college spring break in a VW van with my roommate and another girlfriend have me shaking my head. We sprawled out in the back if it looked like rain, or out on the ground on fair nights. Betty taught us to cook over a camp stove, and we found a small mountain lake with nobody around where we skinny-dipped and sunbathed nude until we were startled by a loud *crack* in the woods. Shrieking with laughter, we covered up only to discover a bull elk staring at us across the water.

Could I manage sleeping in the Jeep almost forty years later? I may have to. But for now, I can stop worrying about my finances and *do* something about them.

I save my budget worksheets and switch to the manuscript I'm being paid to review. Taking just a minute to grab a couple of ibuprofen from my bag and to splash my face with cool tap water, I sit down again, ready to work.

***

The motel's "continental breakfast" includes coffee, white bread, donuts that feel hard enough to use as weapons, and those little plastic packets of jelly. I suppress my craving for scrambled eggs or even a simple bowl of cereal, and carry one load of my belongings to the parking lot. I'd like to get an early start so I can make it to a mountain town in Colorado before dark tonight. For the first time since fleeing the hurricane, I feel a sense of excitement and anticipation, and find myself humming "On the Road Again" as I cross the motel parking lot.

"Oh no. No, no, no!"

Shattered glass sparkles on the blacktop as I step closer to my vehicle. The rear wiper blade dangles like a broken limb beneath a huge gaping hole surrounded by a ragged outline of glass crisscrossed with a complex maze of cracks.

The blanket I used to cover my belongings hangs half out the back, covered with shards. I peer inside and moan as I realize that almost everything that was in the back of the SUV is gone. As I circle the car, I discover both doors on the passenger side are wide open and another window is broken. On the ground, I encounter two of my boxes, torn and mostly empty, several random articles of clothing scattered on the ground, and worst of all, my photo albums broken and torn where they've been dumped. Trembling, I peer inside the car. There's a gaping hole where the radio and display console should be. The glove box is open and all the junk we had stashed in there seems to be strewn on the floor and passenger seat. I spot the envelope where I kept my registration and insurance card. It's been ripped open, but I locate those crumbled papers on the floor. Another envelope where I kept about eighty dollars in emergency cash is nowhere to be found.

I step back and stare at the damage, then turn and survey the parking lot and wall of windows facing the area. Surely *someone* saw or heard something from their motel room. I gather up as many of my belongings as I can manage, and stumble back to the front desk.

"My car's been broken into!" I announce to the desk clerk and three people in the tiny breakfast area next to it. "Somebody smashed out two windows and stole almost everything." I swallow hard, praying I don't burst into tears in front of all these strangers, although my voice is cracking.

"Whoa. That's a bummer," the young man behind the counter manages, before turning back to focus on his computer screen. I turn toward the others and one couple is heading for the door, cups of coffee in hand. The third – a middle-aged, balding man with a handlebar mustache – is staring blankly at me, his mouth actually hanging open.

I turn back to the counter. "Jason," I say, noting his nametag, "can't you help me? Did you see or hear anything suspicious during the night? Maybe you can ask guests who come in for breakfast if they witnessed the break-in?"

It feels like it takes him a full minute to break his focus from his damn computer monitor. "Nope, didn't hear anything. If anyone reports something, I'll let you know. Did you call a glass place yet to come fix it?"

I let out a puff of frustration. "I hadn't even thought that far ahead. I guess I should start by calling my insurance company."

Jason nods. "Yeah. If they ask you which glass company to use, tell 'em Woody's Auto Glass. Sometimes I've seen them get here in less than an hour, and they're good about cleaning up the broken stuff off the pavement. I think I've got a card here somewhere," he says as he pulls open a drawer and sorts through it.

Now my mouth is hanging open. How often does somebody break into a guest's car?

"Yeah. Here you go."

I take the business card he hands me and stuff it into a pocket. "I guess we should report this to the police. Should that call come from you, since it happened on hotel property, or ... ?"

"Nah. If you wanna call the police, that's up to you. But I can tell you, they're not going to do anything but take your information over the phone. It takes something a lot more exciting than a car break-in to get them out here."

Oh, great. I sure know how to pick a hotel.

Back outside, I consider my situation. Nearly all of my clothes are gone or ground into the oily pavement. My basic collection of cooking supplies, silverware, and 30-year-old Corelle plates and bowls – gone. The framed photo of a mountain lake – my favorite – gone. And my photo albums!

I pick up every loose picture, every torn page, my eyes blurring with tears and my back screaming at me each time I lean over.

Damn it! I shouldn't have to be dealing with this alone. Or the goddamn hurricane, and packing our belongings, and escaping across the country. Franklin should have been here to help! We were supposed to be partners for life. For better, for worse, and if this isn't one of those *for worse* times, I don't know what is. A toxic churning of anger and rage and self-doubt overwhelms me – a tidal wave of emotions that have often threatened to drown me over the past eight months. I lean against the car and press my fists against my eyes, fighting to slow my breathing and calm my pounding chest.

Three-and-a-half hours later, I'm emotionally drained, but I have new rear and side windows and plenty of empty space inside my SUV. As Jason predicted, the police never showed up. So much for bad luck *only* happening in threes. My supply seems endless.

On a positive note, there's more than enough room in the back of my vehicle for me to sleep if I need to. With that thought, I locate a sizeable thrift store and purchase a narrow, blow-up mattress that's only slightly shorter than I am and a pillow that doesn't seem to be in too bad of shape. Next, I hit up Walmart and come away with three shirts, two pairs of pants, socks, a bra, and a 6-pack of underwear in an assortment of colors and patterns.

As Franklin would likely have said – if the jackass had been here – I needed this like a goldfish needs a root canal.

Chapter 4

An old-fashioned bell tinkles as I step into the registration office. I had planned to drive much farther today, reaching Pueblo or Colorado Springs before dark, but with the mess with my car this morning and my lengthy stop along the highway to let my melt-down run its course, I decided to pull into what seems to be the one and only lodging choice in this tiny town on the eastern plains of Colorado. I'm relieved to find that the lobby looks as neat and well cared-for as the exterior of the building. Old-fashioned, but homey.

A plump woman emerges from the back, a toothy smile on her face. "Well, hello honey! Welcome to Gadway's Getaway. I'm Wendy Gadway. What can I do you for?"

"I need a single room for one night."

"Sure thing, hon," she says with a chuckle. "As you might have noticed from the parking lot, we aren't exactly full up. Now, would you like a suite with a kitchenette, or just a regular room?"

Since the few food supplies I had were stolen, and figuring there isn't much of a grocery store in a town this size, I opt for the "regular" room.

"Traveling alone?" she asks. Before I can reply, she continues. "You know, I admire women who are brave like that, driving across the country all by their lonesome. I noticed your plates are from South Carolina, so that's why I'm thinking you've maybe come all this way. On vacation or is this a business trip?"

Figuring that "running away from home" would come across as snide, I consider some other response. "Relocating. Hurricane Janelle convinced me I don't want to live near a coast again."

"Oh my. Was your home hit?"

I nod, as an online video I watched repeatedly at Hank's house replays in my mind. It was taken about a mile from my apartment complex, showing the damage to the shopping center where I normally bought groceries. The parking lot was a rushing river of mud and debris, cars and entire trees floating past. An aerial shot, which I paused and studied obsessively, showed homes poking their roofs above a vast lake like a smattering of islands. With few visible roads or highways, I couldn't be sure where the images were taken, but the narrator indicated I might be looking right at my own neighborhood.

"It doesn't matter. There was nothing left there for me anyway. This was a good, hard nudge for me to pack up and move somewhere I'd rather be."

She nods, her face brightening. "So, all the way from the east coast! And where are you moving to? I'm guessing you didn't set out to move here to Wilaka!"

We laugh at this together. Even though I lived in metro Denver for a number of years, it never dawned on me that it was possible to drive across so much of the eastern part of the state and still not catch even a glimpse of the mountains. I was so looking forward to seeing the snowy caps of high peaks – even this time of year – and the spectacular panorama of the Rockies stretching across the western horizon. So far, my home state looks a heck of a lot like the flat wheat fields of western Kansas. More silos and water towers and hardly any trees except where people have planted some within the scattered towns.

"Actually, I haven't decided where I'll settle down. I'm planning on just traveling around a bit and hopefully I'll get it figured out."

I park my Jeep directly in front of the door to my room, which isn't a problem since there is only one other car in the lot. Opening the door, I step inside and let my eyes adjust. Like the front office, the room is decorated with simple but pleasing colors, and appears to be spotlessly clean and well-kept. After transferring everything I own from the car into the room – something I manage easily with two loads – I close and lock the door and sprawl out on the bed.

Surely I can't have any more disasters coming my way. I'm a good person. I give to charity and volunteer at the hospital gift shop. Why do these things keep happening to me?

Why did my husband of nearly forty years suddenly up and leave me? For the millionth time, I search my memory for a clue, for any signs he was unhappy in our marriage. Sure, we had our ups and downs, just like any couple. But we didn't have any ongoing issues – not that I was aware of – and had settled into retirement for him and near-retirement for me far more smoothly than I'd heard for some other couples. Franklin seemed content tinkering with electronics, having time for reading the history books he so enjoyed, taking pickle-ball lessons with me and playing twice a week. He was talking about volunteering as a referee for a local kids' basketball league. We both signed up for adult ed classes at the local community college for next term.

And then he declared that he was leaving and that it had nothing to do with me.

How can that possibly be true? Our lives have been intertwined for four decades. We've shared joys and sorrows, confided in each other, loved each other. Together, we faced the disappointment of being unable to have children, the thrill of a big promotion at his work, and the publication of my first major magazine article. How can he end all that and refuse to talk about what's going on?

I decide a long, scalding-hot shower is what I need right now.

When I emerge, I can't avoid my reflection in the full-length mirror. When did I turn into such a frumpy, lumpy, saggy old woman? And how did I not really notice until now?

"Because you don't have a single full-length mirror at home, that's why," I announce to the empty motel room.

Maybe Franklin got sick of looking at me. Although he certainly hasn't kept his "boyish figure" over the years, either, and I still find him attractive. Could his reason for leaving be as shallow as that? Of course, I'm all too aware that I've added extra pounds since he's been gone, bingeing on junk food for comfort. Which never actually comforted me.

I pull on a t-shirt so I don't have to look at my rolls of fat and focus on blow-drying my hair. I fuss with the roots I can see, distressed to see how much silver is showing. At some point, I'll look for a salon for a touch-up, but I'll just have to live with this for now. Having hardly eaten anything all day, I flip through a three-ring binder of information for motel guests, looking for a place to go out to dinner. I conclude that the Wilaka Diner may be the only game in town.

With the diner being only two blocks from the motel, I choose to walk. Thankfully, I'm on the shady side of the street, since it feels like it must still be in the 90s. Spotting my destination, I pause. None of the charm and coziness of

Gadway's Getaway has been achieved for the Wilaka Diner. It's desperately in need of a paint job, and weeds are growing out of the cracks in the sidewalk in front of its entrance. The "Wil" in "Wilaka" is almost illegible. But there's a neon "Open" sign blinking in the front window, which is either frosted or simply too filthy to see through.

With a sigh, I ease the screen door open and try to peer inside, needing time for my eyes to adjust to the change in lighting.

"Come on in!" a woman, no more than a dark outline, calls out to me. "Just sit anywhere you like. I'll be right with you." She bustles toward the back and I glance around the room now that I'm starting to be able to see. It looks better than I expected. Kind of run-down, with duct tape covering rips in most of the vinyl booth seats, and a noticeable chip off the top of the first table I pass, but my impression is that it is clean.

I was hoping to look over a menu before committing to eat here, but since the menus are tucked behind the napkin dispensers on each booth, I select a seat that seems to be in decent shape and slide in, grunting with the effort of scooting in far enough to grab a menu.

My focus gravitates to the dessert list first. Apple or cherry pie a la mode, chocolate cake, ice cream sundaes. My mouth starts to water. I skim the dinner choices, lingering over the meat loaf with mashed potatoes and gravy, the chicken-fried steak – also with mashed potatoes – and, not surprisingly, the deep-fried chicken with, you guessed it, mashed potatoes and gravy.

As I consider these choices, I hear the hostess / waitress greet two women who have just entered the restaurant and glance their way. Both look to be in their sixties, but I say that simply because of their graying hair and the lines on their faces. One is quite tall, with her hair in two braids hanging just below her shoulders. She's thin and muscular. The other is about my height, with very short, spiky hair, and is somewhat hefty, yet without seeming at all fat. Just powerful. They're both wearing skin-tight bicycling shorts and colorful, short-sleeved jerseys, and carrying helmets under an arm.

They may be turning gray, but they are the fittest-looking women I think I've ever seen in person, different as they are from each other. Energy seems to pour off them as they virtually float to a booth across the room and gracefully glide into their seats.

I realize I'm staring, so I drop my eyes to my menu again. What would it feel like to be strong and fit like those two? To look in the mirror and see myself as an energetic and confident woman? To flaunt my gray hair like a crown of honor?

When the waitress comes to take my order, I request the grilled chicken breast with steamed broccoli off the "Lighter Fare" section of the menu.

It's not about Franklin. After all this time, I don't believe he's coming back and honestly I don't know if I'd take him back if he did show up. This is about me. I'm tired of being tired. I've started on this journey and I'm ready to redefine myself.

If Franklin can run away to find himself, so can I.

Chapter 5

Just when I'm beginning to wonder if the mountains will ever come into view, I spot them as the highway crests a small rise. A feeling of joy sweeps over me as I reach my first actual goal – to revisit the beautiful Rocky Mountains of my youth!

After wending my way through the populated Front Range cities, I sigh with pleasure as the road becomes more curvy, paralleling the river in a valley surrounded by granite walls. As the highway climbs, the outside temperature moderates and I roll down my windows to enjoy the temperate breeze and the whiff of evergreens. My excitement grows as my GPS instructs me to turn left in 1,000 feet. I finally feel like my adventure is beginning. I'm ready to settle into a mountain campground and just relax for a while, surrounded by nature.

I ease my Jeep into the entrance of Far Away Campground and stop in front of the office. It takes me a minute to stand upright and release the kinks from my legs. I was so excited to get here that I took very few breaks from driving today, so this is the price I pay. Soon, though, I hobble inside to register for a campsite.

"Hi there. I'm Margie. How many nights will you be staying with us?"

I smile down at the woman sitting at a computer behind the counter. "How about I pay for three nights now and maybe extend that later?"

She frowns slightly. "I can give you the weekly rate if you reserve a full week right up front. If you take the daily rate, you'll spend more for six nights then you would for the full seven." She hands me a rate schedule and points to the figures with her pen.

"Okay, then. I'll go for the whole week," I say, smiling at the weekly amount. I paid almost that much for a single night at the budget hotel where most of my belongings were stolen.

"Now, you understand there are no hook-ups. But we have very nice bathrooms and showers, a laundry, and a picnic area. There's water just a short ways beyond your site, so it's real convenient." She sits up taller and peers out the window. "Oh, sorry. I thought you had a camper. You'll see that there's a nice, flat spot for your tent. Do you need firewood? Each site has a designated fire pit."

Firewood? A small campfire might be fun. I remember roasting marshmallows on long sticks when I was a kid, pulling a flaming, gooey mess from the fire and smashing it between two Graham crackers with a square of milk chocolate. But I don't recall ever building a fire myself, and I don't expect I'll discover I have a knack for doing so. "No thanks," I say before another thought hits me. "Um, is there a kitchen or really just a stove that I can use to heat up my dinner?" Didn't Lorraine from my Book Club talk about a communal kitchen she and her friend used when they went on that camping trip in Vermont?

The woman shakes her head. "Sorry. We don't have anything like that. You don't have a camp stove?"

I feel heat rising to my face. "Not yet. I was planning on buying one on the way here, but didn't get a chance to." I clear my throat and lean on the counter, trying to look comfortable and casual. "Are there any towns nearby where I might get one?"

To her credit, she suppresses an incredulous look on her face nearly before I detect it. "Well, I think the closest would be either the ranch supply or the camping store in Salida. One of them should stock propane camp stoves and the canisters. You could pick up a cooking pot and maybe a frying pan, too. How're you set for plates and bowls and utensils?"

I feel like a total dunce. I don't have *anything* for cooking or eating meals. I can't imagine the thieves have found any use for my kitchen items they stole. I picture them dumped in a field somewhere in Kansas, crushed under the hooves of a herd of cows.

"Thanks for your help, Margie," I say, studying the campground map to see where I need to go to reach my site.

As I step out the door, she calls after me. "Let us know if there's anything else you need. Enjoy your stay!"

Pulling into my spot, I cut the engine and step outside, inhaling deeply. The woods are lovely and offer a sense of privacy, although I know there's a tent set up in the next campsite and a small camper of some sort on my other side, both mostly hidden by forest vegetation. I turn slowly in a full circle, taking it all in. After creeping through traffic escaping the storm, attempting to sleep in a crowded church basement, staying with Hank in a busy suburb, then driving for days across the Midwest and Great Plains, it feels wonderful to simply stop and relax. I have no appointments, nobody expecting anything of me.

I also have no tent and no way to cook the simple foods I purchased earlier today. I don't even have a can opener or spoon to allow me to eat my damn cold chili straight from the can like a hobo. What was I thinking? It's late in the day and the last thing I want to do right now is jump back in the car and drive forty-five minutes each way to shop for all the things I'm going to need to make this week-long camping stay work. There was a tiny café right where I turned off the highway. That's less than ten minutes from here. And I can just eat one of my breakfast bars in the morning, then deal with finding the items I need.

I start a shopping list for tomorrow. Camp stove and fuel, lighter, pot and pan, coffee mug, bowl, plate, eating utensils, kitchen knife, can opener. I bought one of those Styrofoam coolers at the grocery store earlier today, but now I'm wondering if I'll need something more substantial. Ice. Fresh vegetables? Ready-made salads?

I write down "cookies" but then scratch it off, thinking of those fit cyclists at the diner last night. Inspired by that thought, I lock my car and set off to walk around the campground loop, imagining that this will be the first of many hikes I will take while I'm here. I set off at a rapid clip, but a stitch in my side slows me almost immediately.

Oh well. Rome wasn't built in a day. I stroll slowly along the gravel drive, checking out the tents and RVs in the campground. I stop to watch as a woman stands at the back of a site, gesturing to her partner who is attempting to back their camping trailer into position. "No!" she shouts. "Can't you see me in the mirror? You need to pull *that* way." She stabs her arm to her right repeatedly. The man yells something I don't quite make out, then pulls forward. They begin their dance again, but I realize she has noticed me watching and clearly isn't happy about that, so I offer a timid wave and continue on my way. "Roger! I told you to move to your left! Turn the other way!" Her voice fades as I hurry off, moving as fast as I can without getting another cramp in my side.

By the time I've completed the loop, I'm breathing hard and my legs ache. I plop down at the picnic table in my campsite to catch my breath and rest. Finally, I push myself to my feet and look around for the water supply that Margie at the front office described, picturing a drinking fountain. Instead, I discover a water spigot where you raise a handle and water pours out a spout. I return to my car and dig out my shopping list, adding "Water containers – small and large."

It's only 5:00 p.m., but my walk made me quite hungry, so I climb into my vehicle and head back to the main highway to have dinner.

The diner has a very rustic, log cabin décor with antique knickknacks dangling from the ceiling, sitting upon a shelf high above the tables, and tacked to the walls. Old-fashioned snowshoes and ski equipment are surrounded by dented cans of coffee, tobacco, baking powder, and spices, colorful old glass bottles, and signs declaring that Horse Thieves will be Hung and Please Check Your Guns at the Door.

I flip open the menu and scan it quickly. Expecting the Old West theme to be continued with the food offerings, I'm surprised that the largest portion of the menu is dedicated to German dishes. *Bratwurst, Wiener Schnitzel, Sauerbraten*. I locate the section for *Salads*, but nothing sounds satisfying. Another category is called *Kummerspeck*, which includes an explanation for the term. "*Kummerspeck* can be thought of as *Comfort Food*. The literal translation is *Worry Bacon*. Let our *Kummerspeck* dinners ease your sorrows and stress."

Bacon is featured prominently in each of the selections. There's a Bacon and Cheese Quiche (do Germans make a good quiche?), Bacon Burgers, and a Bacon-Wrapped Steak. My mouth is watering.

Oh, hell. I need to treat myself tonight, since it's my first night camping. What was that old saying? Today's the first day of the rest of your life? So, make that tomorrow. Tonight I'm celebrating with quiche. And chocolate lava cake for dessert. Tomorrow, I'll walk twice around the campground loop and eat a salad for dinner.

As I climb back into my SUV, I glance up at a couple just entering the restaurant. His back toward me, he holds the door for her and my breath catches. Thick, white hair above broad shoulders – could that be Franklin? My heart thunders until he turns so I can see him in profile. Other than his general build and white hair, this man doesn't even resemble my errant husband.

I close my eyes and breathe deeply. I thought I had stopped doing this. Stopped looking for Franklin in places he'd never be. With another sigh, I start my engine and head back to Far Away Campground.

**

The warmth from earlier this afternoon has faded now that the sun has dipped below the mountains surrounding the valley. I set up my laptop and sit at the picnic table for a short time, attempting to focus on making progress with the book I'm proofreading, but I'm soon distracted by the chill in the air. When I had my little shopping spree in Kansas to replace some of my stolen clothes, it was easily 95° outside – it never dawned on me to buy a light jacket or even a sweatshirt. Retrieving my blanket from the back of the car, I shake it out for the umpteenth time, trying to make sure no broken glass remains hidden in its fibers before I wrap it around my shoulders. Making my final trip to the restroom before I settle in for the night, the people in the site next door watch me from their camp chairs and wave politely as I walk by. Mason and Janice Hollander are their names, I learn as I pass the cute sign they've hung outside their unit. I wave back.

In the ladies' room, I change into my summer-weight pajamas – the only ones I still possess. Feeling incredibly self-conscious, I hurry back to my campsite, wrapped in my blanket for modesty yet feeling the cool night air chilling my exposed legs. I crawl into the back of my vehicle, feeling like a contortionist as I pull the back hatch closed behind me. Earlier, I put down the rear seats and moved all my belongings to one side, other than my wimpy air mattress and pillow. It takes a considerable amount of twisting and grunting, yanking and pushing, for me to get the blanket arranged over me and to find a position where my feet aren't dangling off the bottom edge of the pad. By the time I have everything in place, I'm panting like I ran a marathon.

But at least I'm warm. Actually, as I notice this, I recognize the heat ascending from my core, like hot water rising rapidly up through my torso and into my head. "Damn!" I sputter, grabbing the top of the blanket and holding it straight up above me so cooler air can reach my flushed body. "When are these damn hot flashes ever going to go away?!" At least they aren't as bad as they were in the couple of years before my periods finally ended – which was almost a decade ago.

Finally, my body finishes emitting heat and I lower the blanket around me before I become chilled. Franklin used to joke that Global Warming wasn't caused by man – women were to blame. All of us female Baby Boomers hitting menopause at the same time with our hot flashes were at fault. I used to think that was funny.

It's surprisingly bright out, considering the only lights I've seen are by the bathroom doors. I roll onto my side so my face is almost pressed against the back passenger door and try to relax. I hear a series of tones, a pause, and the sounds repeat. An owl? There's a creaking sound – rather faint, but noticeable in the extreme silence of the woods – that comes and goes with no obvious pattern. My eyes pop open and I turn my head to look out the windows at the sky above me. Ah, it's the trees. A breeze has come up and the branches are swaying.

I must have finally dozed off, because I'm startled by someone shining an intense light in my eyes. Frightened, I cry out, "Go away! Leave me alone!" before I shake off my drowsiness and realize it's just the nearly-full moon glaring through the car window. Not needing my flashlight, I'm able to locate a t-shirt which I drape over my eyes after repeating my earlier contortions to untangle myself from my blanket and get everything arranged again.

Long before the sun begins to lighten the sky, I'm awake again, curled into the fetal position in an attempt to stay warm. I've layered a t-shirt and a pair of pants over my PJs and pulled on two pairs of socks. Not owning a cap, I've covered my head with a pair of brand-new panties. I need to pee something awful, but the thought of extracting myself from the relative warmth of my car and walking a hundred yards to the bathroom in the chilly breeze is almost inconceivable. Please, don't let me pee myself. If I freeze to death like this, it will be totally humiliating, but then again, I'll never know it.

Finally, my bladder aching, I manage to squeeze my feet into shoes, wrap the blanket around me, and shimmy out of the car without wetting my pants. I encounter a couple walking their dog as I traipse as swiftly and smoothly as I can to the restroom. They grin and greet me as we pass, and I can hear them snickering once they're behind me. Is my desperation to pee that obvious? Dashing into a stall, I nearly cry with relief once I take care of my business.

The sink only offers cold water for washing. As I glance up at my image in the mirror, I groan in embarrassment. Pale pink panties with green polka dots still cap my head. I yank them off and stuff them in my pocket, then finger-comb my hair. The good news is that the bathroom is equipped with one of those warm air hand dryers, so I run it through repeated cycles, reawakening my chilled hands and arms, turning the air nozzle upward to blow on my upper body and face. When a young lady in shocking pink Dora the Explorer pajama bottoms, Mickey Mouse bedroom slippers, and an enormous orange parka walks in the door, I decide most anything goes when sharing a bathroom with dozens of strangers. I chuckle to myself all the way back to my car.

Chapter 6

I spread out my new purchases on the picnic table and step back to admire them. After visiting the farm supply store, then the camping goods place, then back to the farming store again after my sticker shock, I feel that I've struck a fair balance between purchasing things I need and avoiding spending so much that I'll have to eat nothing but ramen noodles for the rest of my life.

My new sleeping bag won't cut it if I try to camp in December in the mountains, but I'm hoping it'll suffice if I'm in southern Arizona by winter. While the coffee press sounded enticing, I'm sure I'll do just fine with the little percolator I picked up. One large pot, one aluminum frying pan, various cooking utensils, and my new prize possession – a two-burner camp stove and a three-pack of small propane canisters.

"Looks like you've been shopping."

The folks from the camper next door have wandered over to check out my display. The man offers a hand to shake. "Hi, there. We're the Hollanders. I'm Mason."

"And I'm Janice."

Which I already knew, of course, because of the sign they've hung for all passersby to see.

"Ellie," I offer, stopping myself before I continue with the introduction I've repeated innumerable times over the years. *We're Franklin and Eleanor, like the Roosevelts. But I just go by Ellie.*

"We wondered how you did last night when we didn't see a tent. Not that people don't sometimes sleep in their vehicles, but when you took off so early this morning, we figured you might have been cold."

Mason nods somberly at his wife's words. "We would have invited you in for a cup of coffee if you hadn't left so quickly."

"That's very kind of you," I say, feeling a blush rise to my cheeks as I recall my panty hat. "I really was short on supplies last night, but I'm hoping I've picked up the things I'll need so tonight will be much more comfortable."

We chat for a little while longer, covering the usual topics most strangers discuss. Where are you from, what kind of work do you do or are you retired? Where have you been traveling before you came to Forever View?

A nonverbal signal seems to pass between them and Mason excuses himself to "take care of something." He retreats to the far side of their camper.

Janice runs her hand along the open lid of my new camp stove, nodding as if she were inspecting a fine sculpture. "If you don't mind my asking, how did you happen to arrive here without hardly any camping supplies?" She focuses directly into my eyes with such a sympathetic look on her face that I feel like she might be psychic. She reaches out and squeezes my shoulder. "Did you have to leave home suddenly?"

Amazed, I nod in confirmation. "How did you know?"

She pats my arm and nods in sync with me. "Ellie, it's sad but a fact of life. Many women have found themselves in a position where they need to leave a dangerous situation.

Just like you, they grab whatever they can and get out before things escalate. I think fate brought us together. I told you I worked as a bookkeeper, but I also volunteered for a number of years at a women's shelter. Believe me, you're not alone. I'm sure I can find some local resources for you, if you're open to that."

Oh, Lord. She thinks I ran away from an abusive husband, not a threatening hurricane. I end up telling her all about fleeing the coast, the church shelter, and the break-in, but omit disasters number one and two in my life – the wildfire and my husband's mysterious Disappearing Act. We've known each other for less than an hour – I don't need to offer up my entire life history.

Once I convince Janice that I am not a victim of domestic violence, she invites me to "happy hour" in front of their camper in twenty minutes. "All we have is wine and beer," she explains, "and some simple snacks. No need to bring anything – this is just something we enjoy doing our last evening at each campground."

Under other circumstances, I would insist on bringing something to the party, but I have no booze and no snacks suitable for sharing, unless I were to slice up the two energy bars the sales person talked me into buying. I hem and haw, "Well, I don't know," which she squelches immediately. "Just come over for a little bit. Meet a few interesting people we've talked to in camp." I acquiesce and thank her for the invitation, realizing how much I've missed having anyone to talk to since leaving Hank and Cheryl's.

I busy myself for the next twenty minutes by stowing all my new belongings and food back inside my Jeep, since I won't have a clear view of my campsite from next door. Pleased with my purchases, I arrange my bed with my new sleeping bag, placing my new knit cap and my blanket within easy reach for the night. I had considered purchasing a foam sleeping pad, since my blow-up didn't do much to cushion my hips or shoulders from the hard surface of my vehicle, but it already seemed like I was spending too much. Maybe the added padding of the sleeping bag will do the trick.

Hearing people greeting one another, I lock the Jeep and wander over to the gathering.

"Hey, there," a man with a scrubby salt-and-pepper beard and a receding hairline says as I approach, "I'm Bob. And you are...?"

"Ellie," I say, shaking his offered hand. His grip is almost painful.

"New to camping, I gather. Now, don't worry about that – we all had to start off somewhere. Me, I starting camping when I was about this high." He holds his hand next to his thigh. "I'm a Full Timer now – been on the road for going-on seven years. Can't imagine going back to living in one place."

He talks too loudly for my taste. He reminds me of one of Franklin's co-workers from about twelve years ago. I'll bet Bob was a salesman, too. Not one of the successful ones, like my husband – relying on knowledge of his field and building true rapport with the client, listening and finding a way to fill their needs. No – more like the sort of guy who dominates every conversation and does everything "big." Big voice, big talk, overly friendly – the stereotypical used car salesman. As I recall, that co-worker didn't last long.

I'm rescued from Bob with the arrival of Cindy and Lynetta, two elementary teachers from Arizona who are traveling for the summer in a fancy camper van. In appearance, they couldn't be much different. Lynetta is a freckled-faced, ultra-pale redhead, just plump enough that it's easy to imagine her young students glorying in hugs from their smiling teacher. Cindy is African American, tall and lean, with a glorious smile which she shares easily with our small gathering. But what they have in common are their warm and welcoming personalities, which even seem to have an effect on Bob. As we all visit, his overblown demeanor begins to fade, and a more natural persona starts to emerge.

"Where do you plan to go next, Ellie?"

I'm the only one who hasn't shared any details about my journey. I've repeated my quick overview of leaving the east coast and my choice not to return there, but glossed over everything else. The fact is, I've been poring over maps but don't have any better idea of where I want to go when I leave Far Away.

"Maybe somewhere that's a little warmer at night," I reply, then smile bravely. Everyone laughs.

"We came here precisely because it stays so cool, especially at night. Have you ever been to southern Arizona in July?" Lynetta asks. "If we can stay above 7,000 feet elevation the whole summer, we'll be as happy as ducks in a pond."

"You got yourself a warm enough bag?" Bob asks. "It got down to 43° last night – might drop below 40° tonight. It seems like women sleep colder than men – especially their feet – so even a 40° sleeping bag might not be enough."

The guy at the outdoor recreation shop tried to explain temperature ratings of sleeping bags to me, but all I figured out from that lecture was that I didn't want to spend the kind of money they were asking for the bags he was showing me. I went back to the ranch supply store and bought something I felt I could afford. The packaging never mentioned a temperature.

"I'm sure I'll be okay tonight," I answer. "Although I was pretty cold last night. I even wore underwear as a cap to try to stay warm." *I can't believe I just said that out loud.*

Everyone roars with laughter at my confession, and Mason refills my wine glass and offers a toast. "To camping stories!"

Cindy passes me the plate filled with cheese and crackers. "If you're going to be traveling around indefinitely, have you considered getting yourself a camper van? Or a trailer like theirs?" she asks, pointing to the Hollander's camper beside us.

"We love ours," Lynetta adds. "We've got a two-burner stove, a small refrigerator / freezer, a comfortable bed, even a microwave, but that only works when we have shore power."

Seeing my baffled frown, she explains, "Shore power just means that we have a place to plug in for electricity."

"We also have a heater. And a sink with running water, even at a campground like this without a hookup, since there's a water storage tank."

Cindy jumps in. "And a porta-potti. And a table to eat at. And a shower."

"Wow. I had no idea a van could hold all that."

"Tour time!" Bob declares, jumping to his feet. "Follow me."

We parade behind him as he leads us to the end of the loop where his unit is parked. It reminds me of a Greyhound bus, only not nearly as long. Sizable rectangular compartments have emerged from the body of the vehicle on both sides, which I learn are called – appropriately enough – "slide outs." Inside, the place resembles a compact apartment, complete with a couch, booth-style dining table, an enormous flat-screen TV, a kitchen with a decent-sized refrigerator, counter space, cabinets, and double sinks, a tiny bathroom with a step-in shower, and a queen-sized bed that looks just like one you'd have in your house. I'm blown away.

We can even manage to move around with all six of us inside at once.

"I'm amazed! This is nicer than our first apartment just after we got married," I say, then wish I could take it back.

"Oh," Bob says, "I didn't realize you were married. Or ... are you still?" He glances at my unadorned left ring finger and then gazes at me with puppy-dog eyes.

Oh, great. Just when I decide he's an okay guy after all, I realize he's *interested* in me. Nope, nope, nope. No way.

"It's complicated," I say, stepping toward the door. "So, who's next on the tour?"

We visit the two teachers' impressive camper van and I imagine myself traveling in luxury in a vehicle like it. While I can't fathom being able to maneuver a motorhome like Bob's, the van seems manageable to drive. As the others spread out, peering in through the sliding side door and the back, and examining the van from all sides, I quietly pull Cindy aside.

Keeping my voice low, I ask, "If you don't mind my asking, about how much does a camper like this cost?"

My heart sinks when she gives me a figure. Seeing the expression on my face, she chuckles. "That's why we're *renting* it for the summer. We got lucky – our assistant superintendent is charging us a fraction of what we'd pay someone else. She and her husband took it on sabbatical last year and now they're buying one of those mega-motorhomes for when he retires from his medical practice in September."

"Will they sell this one?"

She sighs. "Yeah. But I already asked about the price and it's still way out of my range. Are you thinking you might be interested?"

"Interested, yes, but unless we're talking about a 90% off sale, I can't even think about it."

We finish our tour of camping homes back at the Hollanders' trailer, which is sized mid-way between Bob's motorhome and the ladies' van. Although roomier than the van, I gather it is the least expensive of the lot.

"Yep, you need to get yourself a camper of some sort," Bob says. "I see that sparkle in your eyes."

"Once you sleep, and cook, and eat in one of these, you'll never want to go back to sleeping in the back of your car and cooking outside in the rain and wind," Janice adds.

That's all well and good, but unless someone gives me a camper as a gift, I may as well forget about it.

"Speaking of cooking," Cindy says, "I think we'll go start dinner. Thanks for the goodies." She and Lynetta hug everyone goodbye and depart. Bob turns to leave, but he spins back and hands me what appears to be a business card.

"Hey, here's my contact info. I meet a lot of people when I'm traveling around and I might have a lead on a great deal on a little camper trailer if you're interested."

I study the card for a moment. "That's very kind of you, but I don't really know what my plans are, travel-wise. And the thought of pulling a trailer scares me. But thanks all the same."

"Well, if you change your mind ..." Tentatively, he sticks out his hand to shake mine. Feeling grateful for his kindness and just a little guilty for my initial negative impression of him, I give him a brief hug.

"I'll think about it," I say.

I give my regards to Mason and Janice for their hospitality and return to my campsite, where I decide it's time to try out my new purchases. After filling up my new two gallon water carrier, I carefully follow the instructions for my new, handy-dandy coffee percolator. While that heats up over one burner on my easy-peasy stove, I measure out enough water to prepare the intriguing freeze-dried camp dinner I bought, much to the amusement, I believe, of the very young man who waited on me at the outdoor equipment store.

"Okay, so if you've been out hauling a seventy-pound backpack for ten hours, these babies are going to taste incredible," he explained. "But for car camping, like you're doing – well, not so great."

Still, I was fascinated by the vacuum-packed pouches labeled with a variety of entrée names that would make a restaurant proud. Pouches that weighed almost nothing. Turkey Tetrazzini, Chicken Teriyaki, Beef Stroganoff, Lasagna, Pad Thai, and even Key Lime Pie and Apple Crisp. I'm being good. Instead of one of the desserts, I've selected Pasta Primavera, since it sounds like something with lots of heathy vegetables.

I carefully pour boiling water into the stand-up pouch, stir, reseal it, and wait the appropriate number of minutes. I peer inside and frown at the clumps. Stir again, more thoroughly this time, add a touch more hot water, and give it another minute. Peek inside again – better.

Now for the taste test. Although the instructions say you can eat directly out of the pouch, I think the steam will burn me if I try dipping my normal-length fork into the deep container, so I pour it all into my new bowl. And stir again. Lifting a bite to my lips, I blow to cool it and take a taste.

It's not too bad. Nothing I'll prepare again, mind you, unless I find myself lugging a huge backpack all day and want to carry a meal that weighs almost nothing, but it's okay. I try a few more bites, then pour the rest back into the pouch, seal it, and deliver it to the dumpster beside the restroom. A little goes a long way.

I consider cooking a real dinner, but realize I'm not actually hungry after all the appetizers and wine I consumed at our little gathering. For a short time, I sit at the picnic table and peruse a book on my e-reader, but my butt goes to sleep before long and my back aches, so I shift to the passenger seat in my car. Unable to keep my eyes open, I prepare for bed despite the early hour. Hopefully I'll get more sleep tonight in my new bag than I did my first night out.

Chapter 7

I'm up much too early again, although I made it through most of the night without freezing. Between my sleeping bag and the blanket, my new knit cap and thick socks, I didn't feel chilled until around 4:30 this morning – 4:26, to be precise. Whether it's the cold or my stiff, aching body that ended my sleep for the night, I soon realize I can't lie here any longer. I extract myself from my bedding, spend about five minutes convincing my body to straighten up, visit the restroom and the wonderful hand dryer, and nest in the front seat of my Jeep wrapped in my blanket, watching the sky gradually lighten. Around 6:30, when I notice lights coming from Mason and Janice's camper next door, I venture outside to fire up my little camp stove to heat up some water for oatmeal and coffee.

Pacing to stay warm as I keep an eye on the stove, the gorgeous aroma of coffee reaches me just before I hear footsteps on the gravel roadway. "Ellie, how about some java? I've brought you an egg sandwich, too. We're cooking up the last of our eggs before we hit the road."

Janice hands me a mug and a plate wrapped in aluminum foil. "Oh, no. I couldn't," I say, overwhelmed by her hospitality, but salivating at the marvelous smells.

"Of course you can," she says. "I apologize that we can't sit down with you for a leisurely breakfast, but we're almost all packed up and heading out. We just have to finish hooking up the trailer. Go ahead – enjoy," she adds as I stand holding her food gifts. "We'll come say goodbye before we pull out."

I thank her and take a sip of the piping hot coffee as she disappears into her camper again. I turn off the burners on my stove, realizing that I had forgotten to pour coffee grounds into my new little percolator, which was just coming to a boil. That would have been a huge disappointment.

After heartfelt hugs and an exchange of email addresses, the Hollanders drive away and I remember how it felt when we fled our California home. Some folks, like the Williamsons, returned and rebuilt. Nan and Peter Uchida moved to San Francisco. Over time, we just fell out of touch with one another, despite all the occasions when we used to get together for barbecues or movie nights. I was barely getting to know Janice and Mason and I can't imagine we'll actually keep in touch once they return to their "real" lives and I figure out what *my* real life should be.

After eating, I remember my pledge to myself to walk around the campground loop twice, so I set out at what feels like a pretty swift pace. That lasts about thirty seconds. Although I got more sleep last night, my body feels like I was digging ditches for hours rather than resting. "What doesn't kill you makes you stronger," I mumble, and hobble on.

I don't know if people are friendlier in the morning or if my desire to pause and chat for a moment every chance I get is written all over my face. I spot the young couple with a dog from yesterday morning – the ones who tried not to laugh out loud at my underwear-for-a-hat getup. They both smile broadly and wave as they stand huddled close together, each sipping from huge mugs. The dog lies in the entrance to their tent and watches the world go by. Pajama girl has her same outfit on this morning, and I see that she and a girlfriend – also in pajama bottoms, but wrapped in a yellow blanket rather than a ski parka – seem to have slept out under the stars. Two bulky sleeping bags lie side-by-side on the ground, but there is no tent in sight.

"Hey, look who's out and about already this morning! Come have a sit."

My feet and I would like nothing better. "Good morning, Bob. Don't mind if I do."

Bob pushes up from his camping chair and unfolds its twin. I suppress an eye roll as I peruse his outfit – a somewhat ratty bathrobe hanging loosely over a t-shirt of indeterminate color, a pair of baggy plaid shorts that reach to his knees, and an unfortunate swatch of bare belly between the two. Slide-in slippers and bed hair complete his ensemble.

"Coffee?" he asks, stepping toward the door of his camper.

"I'd love some."

Moments later, he emerges with a tall mug. We settle into the chairs and I sip contentedly, wiggling my toes and circling my ankles in relief.

"So, I've been thinking about our conversation last night," he starts.

I offer a puzzled look. "Which one?"

"About what sort of camper you should get."

"I didn't realize we ever talked about that. Sorry if I gave the impression that I'm in the market for a camper. Now, if I won the lottery or someone just decided to give me one, that would be another matter." I snicker and take another sip. Yesterday got me thinking. I'd been curious about the various contraptions we'd see rolling down the freeway or parked in a campground we'd pass on the way to our motel during a trip. I'd always wanted to look inside, to ask people what it was like to have a home that traveled with you. I even suggested to Franklin that we stop at an RV dealership not far from us in South Carolina to look at their units, just for fun. He had no interest whatsoever. I don't know why I didn't just go do it by myself.

"Well, I don't know of anyone giving away their unit," Bob says, pulling his phone out of his bathrobe pocket, "but I may have a lead on a deal that comes about as close as you're likely to get." He swipes his thumb across the screen a few times, squinting at the display. "Unless they've already sold it."

Finding what he was searching for, he hands me the phone. "Isn't that the cutest thing? It's called an A-frame design, for obvious reasons."

I'm familiar with A-frame cabins. From the front, the triangular buildings resemble a capital "A" with steep roof lines ending in a high point. The walls of the little camper in the photo aren't quite as dramatically angled, but the overall shape is still a wide-footed, triangular "A".

"This is a camping trailer?" I ask, seeing a sturdy-looking contraption sticking out one end that looks almost exactly like the front of the Hollanders' camper. A tongue, they called it.

"Sure is," he says, reaching over to show me that I can scroll to more photos. "I met the folks that own this baby when I was camped over near Steamboat Springs a couple weeks ago. They'd been taking it out for four years, but only a week or two each year. Now they're both retiring and decided they're selling their house and going full time in a thirty-five foot motorhome, top of the line." He chuckles. "I wish them the best of luck, but that's a pretty big step, from this sweet little A-frame to a deluxe Class A."

I'm a bit lost in the jargon, but I get the picture. My initial reaction is that they're nuts to sell their house and have nothing to go back to if they decide they don't want to live in campgrounds all the time, but then it dawns on me that I have nothing to go back to. And no clue where I'll be staying next week or next month.

"You say their new camper—"

"Motorhome."

"Okay, their motorhome is thirty five feet long?" He nods. "So, how long is yours?"

He stares at me with a bemused expression on his face, and I quickly look away and focus on the phone again as I realize my unintentional double entendre. Thankfully, he just clears his throat and gives me a straight answer. "She's twenty-six feet. Now, for comparison, this A-frame is just twelve feet long, not counting the tongue. Take a look at the next photo."

I swipe left and view a mid-sized pickup truck towing a flat, rectangular trailer that's shorter than the truck's cab. "I've seen these on the road," I say. "This is the same camper? It folds up?"

Bob takes back his phone and locates a video. "Watch this," he says, and I'm amazed as a woman demonstrates how, with a push here and a lift there, she can transform the low-lying, rectangular trailer into its A-frame shape and back again. It looks pretty straightforward.

"Ellie, if these folks hadn't told me this unit is four years old, I would have guessed they'd just bought it. It's immaculate. They told me they're taking delivery of the new motorhome the first of August, so they'd like to get rid of the A-frame by then. The house is sold and they're renting it back from the new owners until their RV arrives." He leans closer and lowers his voice. "Between you and me, I think they're rolling in dough. Their asking price is already a steal, and I think they might even take less. They seem to have some sentimental attachment to the A-frame and said they want it to go to 'the right people.' I think they'd be real sympathetic to your situation, driven from your home by that storm and all. And selling to a mature, single woman."

I don't correct him. "I'll admit I'm intrigued, Bob, but I really don't know what my plans are, and I'm trying to be very careful with money until I get that all worked out. But thanks for letting me know." I return his phone and push myself upright with a low groan. "And thanks for the coffee."

"Think about it. But don't wait too long. Somebody's going to snatch this baby up."

"I'll do that."

He rises, finally pulling down his shirt to cover his belly. "You know where to find me. Enjoy your day."

Chapter 8

With my folded blanket as a cushion on the picnic table bench, I power up my laptop, anticipating wrapping up my proofreading project within the next hour. It's been a struggle to focus on work with all the chaos in my life, but my client has been extremely understanding. Still, I had hoped to have it completed almost a week ago, so it will be a relief to email it back to her today and, of course, to be able to send her an invoice and know that money will be coming in shortly.

I stare at the warning message on the screen in disbelief. *Your battery is very low. Plug in your PC now.*

"Where the hell am I supposed to plug it in?" I mutter. Shouldn't it have given me a heads up before it got to this point? Then again, why didn't I think about charging it up over the past several days? I make sure it has shut down, close the lid, and cover my face with both hands. *I'm an idiot.*

Hearing footsteps approaching along the campground road, I pull myself together and smile at the woman passing by, three small dogs adorned with matching pink bows and pink toenails, all attempting to wrap her legs up with their leashes like she's a May Pole. "They look like a handful," I say in greeting.

As she unravels herself from the tangle, she chuckles. "I'm convinced they do this on purpose. How're you doing this fine morning? You aren't *working*, are you?"

Rising to my feet and suppressing a groan, I shake my head and point at my closed laptop. "Not today. I forgot to charge it up."

"That's just as well. You shouldn't be working in a place like this," she says, waving an arm in a wide arc to take in the surrounding forest and peaks, the unbelievably blue and cloudless sky. "Shame on you!"

I take in her sparkling necklace and bracelet, dangling earrings, pink fingernails that match those of her dogs, and trendy outfit with a famous logo ostentatiously displayed along one leg. Her yoga pants alone probably cost as much as my monthly rent. I'll bet she's never had to worry about being able to afford a place to live. I barely stop myself from saying aloud what I'm thinking. *Where do you get off telling me where and when I can work?*

Instead, I gather up my computer and my blanket and turn my back on her, heading to my car. "Have a nice day," I call out in a sing-song-y voice that I hope sounds as phony as I intend it to be. I lean into the cab of my vehicle, offering her my broad butt to speak to if she has anything else to add. When I straighten up again, she's gone.

You need people like her like Mahatma Gandhi needs a nuclear arsenal.

Forty years of living with a man, and my mind can't help but conjure up what his offbeat comment might be.

Now, where the hell am I going to charge up my computer? I know there's an outlet in the ladies' restroom next to the sink, since there was a girl there this morning with an arsenal of beauty-care products, a curling iron, and a hair dryer who seemed to be attempting to prepare herself for the Miss America contest. She was just getting started the first time I visited the facilities; still going strong when I returned an hour later after drinking two cups of coffee.

I could plug in there and possibly set the computer on the floor, which strikes me as unsanitary. And then what? Hang around the bathroom for a few hours while it charges up? I'm certainly not going to just leave it sitting in there while I return to my campsite or go for a walk.

A walk? My back and hips ache so much from sleeping in the Jeep these past few nights that it hurts just thinking about walking. The only option that makes any sense is to head back into Salida and find someplace I can plug in and wrap up my work.

While I'm there, I can pick up a few more items I've realized I may need. After I ate my instant oatmeal for breakfast this morning, I was at a loss for how to wash my dishes. For the time being, I just rinsed out my cup, bowl, and spoon with boiling water, but if I'm going to fry up a hamburger for dinner tonight or heat up a can of chili, then what? I considered asking Bob for advice, but it occurred to me that his unit is equipped with a kitchen sink and, I assume, a way to dispose of dirty dishwater. It felt like far too much of an imposition to ask to wash my dishes in his place. So, I spied on the group of five kids camped across the road from me.

Their picnic table is covered with plastic crates, a camp stove like mine as well as another heater of some sort, food items, dishes, and other colorful items I can't identify from a distance. They were all bustling about this morning, crawling in and out of their three tents squashed into their site, two girls and three boys of what I guess college age. After observing them strolling about, forking mouthfuls of food from plates – don't they ever sit down? – I finally spotted what I'd been waiting for. A girl and a boy set off down the road carrying a plastic tub and a large tote where I'd seen everyone deposit their dirty dishes.

I followed at a distance. I wasn't trying to be stealthy – I just couldn't walk nearly as fast as they did. When I realized they were heading to the building where the showers and laundry room were housed, I was puzzled. They disappeared around the side of the building. Were they both planning on going into the men's shower room to do their dishes? What would the girl do, wait for him to hand her the washed items out the door?

When I circled the structure, I discovered the two of them hard at work by an outdoor sink under a prominent sign, "Dishwashing station." When I returned to my camp, I pulled out the information sheet and campground map I was given when I first arrived. Sure enough, if I had just taken the time to study the map I would have known where to wash my dishes.

I locate my note from this morning to buy a plastic tub, dishwashing soap, and a small dish towel. This will be my third trip into town to buy supplies. Yesterday, I picked up shampoo, soap, and a large towel so I could finally take a shower. How many more items am I going to need just to get through my first week of camping? Then again, since I started out with almost no belongings after the break-in, even if I were moving into an apartment, I'd still need to stock up on most of the same things.

With a loud grunt, I pull myself up into the driver's seat and head into town.

***

"One of the best things you can do for an aching back is walk. Some people think you should just lie in bed all the time, but that's really not a good idea. And sitting is the *worst!*"

"I think lying in my so-called bed is exactly why my back hurts." I take my new acquaintance's advice and get back on my feet, reaching behind my lower back to massage it. Penelope is lean and athletic-looking, someone you'd expect to see in a commercial for running shoes or standing on the winner's platform in the Olympics. Outrageously fit.

In fact, she was jogging past my camp when she stopped to introduce herself and offered to show me some stretches to help my back. I was massaging it then just as I am now. She ran off to fetch a yoga mat from her site and returned moments later to coach me through a series of movements that flowed like ballet from her body. I'm sure I looked like a giant tortoise flailing on its shell trying to turn over, but I do feel a bit better than before.

Penelope, a physical therapist "in real life" as she puts it, peers into the back of my Jeep at my sleeping arrangement. "Okay, for a start, try placing a pillow under your knees when you're sleeping on your back, or between them if you're on your side." When I admit that I don't have an extra pillow, she shows me how to use my new bath towel for the same purpose. "This blow-up mattress is way too thin and it's too short for you. I'll write down some ideas on different kinds of sleeping pads that might work a lot better. There may be a store in Salida that sells outdoor equipment. Do you know where Salida is?"

Laughing, I admit to not only knowing how to find the town, but also having become a familiar face at the sporting goods store. It looks like tomorrow will be yet another shopping day. And the hell with the cost – I can't continue spending nights thrashing around, trying to find comfort when my current bedding feels like I'm being tortured. Another week of this and I many never walk again.

Chapter 9

After another miserable night, I depart camp early, timing it so I'll arrive in Salida right about when the stores open. Chugging along the gravel road toward the main highway, I blink repeatedly, trying to sooth my tired, dried-out eyes. Without warning, I detect a flash of motion and I swerve to avoid hitting a deer that has darted into the road. *Bam! Thud!*

What the hell was *that*? As I come to a halt, I spot the animal bounding away into the woods, unharmed. That crash sounded rock-hard or perhaps even metallic. I step outside and peer back down the road, where I notice a sizeable rock – slightly larger than a bowling ball but sharp-sided – lying in the path of where I just drove. I must have run right over it.

I lean over to peek under my vehicle, but my back issues an unmistakable protest. Slowly and painfully, I straighten up and circle the Jeep, checking for any visible damage yet knowing any problem caused by the small boulder may not be obvious from the side.

Hoping for the best, I climb back into the car and proceed slowly. Once on the highway, I pull over to the side after a few miles, turn off the engine, and sit for a minute before pulling forward a car length. When I check the pavement behind the Jeep, I sigh in defeat. Something is leaking. Well, there's not much to be done about that. I don't have a towing service with my insurance, and the Jeep is still functioning, so I'll just keep going and look for a service station once I reach town.

Despite that decision, my worry continues to grow and I repeat my stop and check for leaks pattern two more times before arriving in Salida. By now, the temperature gauge has crept upwards and is approaching the red area on the display. I scan for a gas station, and pull into the first one I spot.

"Sorry, ma'am, but we don't have any mechanics here. We just sell gas and convenience items."

I realize that should have been obvious when I pulled in. There aren't any service bays. Feeling like a bonehead, I get directions for a nearby service shop that might be able to help me, and ease my ailing SUV along the road in slow motion to that business, mouthing "Sorry!" to other drivers as they pass.

***

"It's your radiator. That rock you hit damaged a hose, but you've also got a slow leak. So, we can probably just repair the leak and put on a new hose for you, but ... when's the last time you flushed the radiator?"

"I really have no idea." I know to get the oil changed and the tires rotated, although I probably let those go a bit too long after Franklin left. Actually, I felt kind of proud of myself when I took the car in for those services. But I don't remember Franklin ever mentioning that he had had the radiator flushed.

Jake, the mechanic, nods knowingly, and wipes his hands again on a red rag he pulls from his pocket. "You've got a lot of miles on your Cherokee. You've got quite a bit of corrosion going on which weakened the radiator so that rock was enough to punch a small hole in it. Frankly, given its overall condition, if you plan to drive this vehicle much longer, I'd advise you to replace the radiator."

Jake gives me a quote for replacing versus flushing and repairing and I don't care for either of the numbers. Is he trying to scare me into doing more than is necessary, just because I'm a woman who clearly doesn't know anything about radiators? God, I wish Franklin were here. He always handled car stuff. Maybe I should get someone else to look at it and see if they say the same thing.

"Let me think about this a minute," I tell him and I retreat to the cramped waiting area where I lower myself with a loud sigh onto an orange, plastic chair.

"Excuse me," an elderly man says, leaning toward me from his perch on a chair across from me, "Sorry to be eavesdropping, but may I offer my two cents?" Dressed in well-worn jeans and a too-large flannel shirt, he rests his elbows on his knees for support.

"Please do," I say, welcoming any input to help me sort this out.

"I've been bringing my vehicles here ever since my arthritis got to be too bad for me to do the work myself," he says, and I notice how crippled his hands are, knuckles jutting out at painful angles, many swollen to double the normal size. "I always used to repair all my own vehicles – cars, trucks, tractors, you name it. These guys are good – they know their stuff. They're honest and fair. What he told you about corrosion, that's just the sad truth. You have them just patch up that old radiator of yours, you'll be back in the shop again before you know it, or worse, stuck on the side of a road waiting for a tow. I'd say, unless you're getting rid of that Jeep in the next few months, get yourself a new radiator."

I reach across to him and place my hand over his. "Thank you. I really didn't know what to do."

He sits up again and smiles broadly. "Glad to be of help, young lady."

I snicker at the thought that a sixty-one-year-old woman can qualify as a *young lady*, but given that I'm guessing this gentleman is easily in his late eighties if not older, I simply accept it as a compliment.

All the money I've saved by camping this week instead of staying in a motel will be wiped out by this incident. When will this bad luck streak ever end? I return to the counter and offer my decision to go ahead with the new radiator. "About how long will it take to replace?" I ask, thinking I might walk the three blocks to the sporting goods store to shop for a sleeping pad while they work on it.

Jake frowns. "Well, if we had the right part in the shop, we could probably get that done for you in a couple of hours. But we're going to have to order a radiator from Denver, so..."

"Would anybody else in town have one?" I ask, my stomach starting to sour.

"Well," Jake says, his face already telling me how unlikely it is, "I can call around. But you got to understand, we're not like a big city. There's only one other shop that could possibly carry a radiator for your older model Cherokee. But, if we can't find one in town, we can have a dealer in Denver overnight it here and have your vehicle ready to go by late tomorrow afternoon."

I guess that answers my question about ending my bad luck streak – it's still going strong.

After confirming Jake's suspicion that the part will have to be ordered, I give the okay to the additional overnight shipping charges to be added to my tab. With only a little bit of begging and dishing out my *poor, pathetic woman on my own* spiel, the shop provides me with a tiny, but drivable two-door sedan to use until my own car is ready tomorrow afternoon. I transfer all my worldly belongings from the Jeep to the sedan, barely leaving myself room to fit inside to drive, and head out to go spend even more money on a decent sleeping pad and then find a motel room for the night, since there's no plausible way I can sleep inside my stuffed-to-the-gills borrowed car.

Chapter 10

I'm in heaven! After a long soak in the tub, I slip between the smooth, clean sheets and wriggle like a contented cat into the perfect position. Refusing to worry further about the cost of a motel room and a new radiator, I shut these thoughts from my mind, accepting the fact that I may have to dip into my IRA. Haven't I fretted about finances enough these past eight – no, now its nine – months? It's time to let my guard down, if only for a short while. I'll figure out where I want to land before long, and then I can focus on building up my proofreading business or even finding a local job. I'll work it out.

It takes me a moment when I awaken during the night to remember where I am. My first impulse was to gaze out my car window at the magnificent display of stars visible above the dark campground. Instead, I focus on a small, green light glowing from the smoke detector on the ceiling of my room. Someone is walking – or better described as stomping – around the room above mine. This is followed by the sounds of moving heavy furniture, as best I can guess. I roll toward the nightstand to see the clock glowing 1:42. My upstairs neighbors drag their bed back across the room again as they crush aluminum cans underfoot. While wearing army boots. Or maybe they're playing fetch with their pet rhinoceros. In any case, I'm not getting back to sleep until they settle down.

Despite my discomfort with sleeping in my car; despite spending more time zipping into town to buy supplies rather than relaxing in camp; despite the steep learning curve of figuring out how to cook and clean and bathe without the luxury of a home – despite all of this, it dawns on me that I actually enjoy staying in a campground. I love the fresh smells of the surrounding forest and the calls of the birds from high above in the tops of the trees. I get a kick out of the people around me and delight in how friendly and helpful most have been. The sensation of sweet air in my lungs as I walk around the camp loop lifts my spirits. Each day, I learn something new and discover ways to make the experience more comfortable – well, other than my actual sleeping arrangements, which I'm hoping will improve greatly with my newest purchase.

Not that I wouldn't love sleeping on a mattress like this every night.

I roll over and open my eyes, surprised that it's light enough so I can see everything clearly in my room. Looking at the clock, I calculate that I've been in bed for almost ten hours. I stretch and sit up. I'm still stiff and a bit sore, but the hot bath and a night in a real bed has definitely helped. I treat myself to another hot shower, just because I can, and enjoy a decent assortment of hot and cold selections for breakfast, which is included in my room cost.

After checking out of the motel, I spend my day strolling around town and window shopping, driving to a viewpoint over the river to watch the whitewater rafts float by, and visiting the local library, where I check to see if anyone has posted an inquiry about my proofing and editing services on the professional forums I frequent. Finding nothing new, I post some updates on social media, as I try to do regularly to keep my name in front of people.

By mid-afternoon, although I haven't had a call from the auto shop, I swing by to check on the status of my vehicle repair, and learn that the new radiator has just arrived and the mechanic will be working on my car "soon." I glance out the window at my Jeep which is still parked in their lot and chew on my lower lip, deciding not to quiz them on their definition of "soon." Franklin used to say I'm too accepting. He had more of a "squeaky wheel" approach to customer service, while I'm mostly a "honey rather than vinegar" kind of person. I smile brightly at the man behind the counter. "That's great. I appreciate your getting the part in so quickly and fitting me in. Oh, and loaning me the car to use."

"No problem," he replies before turning to a customer coming in to pick up his vehicle. I retreat to the waiting area, where I sit for several minutes before deciding to walk a few doors down to buy myself an ice cream cone while I wait.

I eat the cone slowly as I sit in a pleasant little park just beyond the ice cream shop. A couple meander by, pushing a toddler in a stroller and herding a slightly older girl in the general direction of a playground. The girl stops to stare at me and runs to catch up with her mother, shrieking, "Ice cream! I want ice cream, Mama!" Now look what I've done. The family changes direction and aims for the ice cream store, the father catching my eye and grinning. He shrugs and mouths, "ice cream" and I laugh.

Checking the time, I decide I've been people-watching long enough so that the repair shop should have made good progress on my car. Walking back, my jaw drops as their parking lot comes into view. My Jeep is still sitting in the exact same spot as before.

Maybe this is good news. Maybe they've finished the job already.

No such luck.

Channeling my inner Pollyanna persona, I approach the service counter with a pleasant smile on my face. "Hi, Ron," I say, reading the name on the young man's shirt. "How are things progressing with my Cherokee?"

He squints at me. "What's your name, again?"

That's not a good sign. "Dwyer. Ellie Dwyer. You're installing the new radiator they overnighted to you from the dealership?"

Turning his attention to his computer, he taps and clicks and squints and types. "Oh. Here it is. Yeah, we'll be getting to it real soon."

I glance at the clock above the door to the work bays, and back at the sign behind the counter that lists their business hours. "I see you usually close at 5 o'clock. Will it be finished by then, or will you guys be working past 5 tonight?"

"Huh," he grunts, looking at the clock. "No. We'll probably be able to pull the old radiator tonight, but it won't be ready for you until noon-ish tomorrow. We've got your number, so we'll give you a call when it's ready."

"Noon? But I thought Jake said it would be done today." My honey tone has definitely taken a turn toward vinegar.

Ron shrugs. "Yeah, well, if the part had been delivered this morning, that might have happened. But it didn't get here till almost 1 o'clock and we had other jobs to finish. So, we'll have it for you tomorrow around noon."

I breathe deeply and consider what I need to do next. "I'm going to need to keep the car you loaned me until then."

"No problem," he says, then retreats through the door to the garage. When I realize he's not returning any time soon, I walk slowly to the door and out to the borrowed car to return to the hotel and book a room for another night. As I pull away, I see my Jeep being moved into a service bay.

"Hi, Jasmine. I'm back," I say to the same desk clerk who checked me into the motel yesterday. "My car isn't ready, so I need to stay again tonight."

"Oh," she says, "that's a bummer."

"I know, but that's the way it is," I say with a smile and a sigh. Thinking of the commotion from my upstairs neighbor during the night, I ask, "Could I get a room on the upper floor?"

"Oh," she says. "I mean, it's a bummer that you need a room tonight. We're like totally full."

"Full?" Of course they are. How could things possibly go right for me?

"Yeah, 'cause there's the river festival this weekend. Sorry."

I had noticed more cars and trucks towing trailers piled high with rafts and kayaks, but I figured it was just a normal weekend phenomenon. "Any suggestions on which places might have a room for tonight?"

Jasmine shakes her head, the long blue hair on the right side of her face falling into her eyes. She tucks the strands behind her ear and my eyes are drawn to the ultra-short area on the left side. I think there's a yin-yang symbol shaved there. "Everybody in town is full. That's what several people have told me this afternoon. They said they'd already checked all the other hotels."

"So, now what do I do?"

Jasmine recommends an RV campground about an hour and a half away that may have very basic cabins for rent. I retreat to my borrowed car and consider my options. I could return to Far Away and ... do what? Throw my new sleeping bag on the ground and sleep under the stars? I shudder just thinking about it. I feel moderately safe inside my Jeep with the doors locked and the windows up at night, but I can't imagine sleeping out in the open, or even inside a tent with nothing but a thin layer of nylon between me and a mountain lion or bear or a person with bad intentions.

Resigned to driving much farther, I call the RV campground and reserve the last of their smallest cabins. The money just keeps flowing away like rafts drifting down a river. Down, down, down.

Chapter 11

I wanted shelter from the weather, and that's about all I have with the cabin. Cute on the outside, extremely basic on the inside, it's a small room with two twin bed frames topped with plastic-coated padding that I hesitate to call "mattresses." Fortunately, with my own pillow and sleeping bag, the setup is an improvement over the back of my car. I still have to walk to the restroom which doubles as a shower area, and there's another spot where I can tote my limited cooking supplies and heat up some soup for dinner.

With time to kill in the morning before returning to Salida, I stroll up and down the rows of campsites, laid out like a parking lot with an occasional tree or shrub between slots. Most of the spaces are filled with enormous motorhomes, slide-outs on both sides threatening to press against the unit next door. Hoses and cords snake from each house-on-wheels to an island of utility services in each site – what I've learned to call "hook-ups." Some people have set up lawn chairs and tables, potted plants, and colorful decorations that hang from awnings over their entry doors and spin in the breeze. Folks smile and wave as I walk past, gawking at their mammoth RVs.

Thinking I'm coming to a vacant gap where someone has already departed, I gasp in delight when I spot an A-frame camper hidden by its giant neighbors. I don't think it is exactly like the one Bob showed me on his phone, but it's certainly quite similar.

It's so cute! It looks like a toy, dwarfed by all these behemoths.

I gape at it, wondering if the owners might be around so I could ask some questions. When the door swings open, I almost turn to leave, realizing they've probably been able to see me staring.

"Hey there," the woman says as she steps down out of the trailer.

"Oh, I'm so sorry. I didn't realize anyone was home. You can't see in at all," I say, pointing at the tinted windows.

"Not a problem."

"Your camper is so cute!" I sound like someone praising an adorable baby.

She grins as she ties back her long hair. "We get that comment a lot. Would you like to see inside?"

"Oh, no. I couldn't impose ..."

A man with his hair tied on top of his head in one of those funny-looking "man buns" pokes his head out the door. "C'mon in. We don't mind a bit." He scrambles outside and, with a broad sweep of his arm, invites me to climb up the two steps as his wife moves inside to be my tour guide. "I'm Cory, by the way, and this is Susanne."

"I'm Ellie. Nice to meet both of you." It takes a moment for my eyes to adjust to the dimmer lighting as I climb aboard. "Oh. It's a lot bigger on the inside than I thought it would be." The photos didn't do it justice, or maybe this camper is larger than the one Bob showed me.

"Yeah, it's our very own TARDIS," the woman says. When I shake my head in confusion, she adds, "Dr. Who?

The spaceship and time machine that looks like a British phone booth from the outside?"

I try to follow what she's saying, but fail.

"Never mind," she says. "So, the couch converts into a queen bed and we can set up another bed here where the table is. It's got a fridge, sink, A/C, microwave, furnace, water storage, hot water heater, two-burner stove ..."

"And headroom," Cory adds, standing on the outside step. "I'm six foot two, and I can stand up to cook or use the sink."

"You seem to really like it."

They both beam. "We love it," they recite in unison.

"What sort of camper do you have?" Susanne asks.

"Me?" I scoff. "I have a Jeep Cherokee that's in the shop, and I sleep in the back. This looks like the lap of luxury compared to living out of my car." I make my way carefully down the stairs to the ground.

"Yeah, we've slept in the back of our van before, but that was when we'd only be out for maybe three or four nights," she says. "Now that we're getting out for a few weeks at a time, this has been great for us. How long are you traveling for?"

I pause, considering my answer. I could say that I'm technically homeless, but that has such a negative connotation. I go for a more upbeat spin. "Until I decide where I want to settle down, I suppose."

"That's so cool," she says. "We're both able to telecommute most of the time, but Cory still has to check back in with his office several times a month, and I need to call on clients at odd times. But in a few years, we hope to be able to travel around even more than we do now."

Suddenly, I hear jazzy music and Cory fishes a phone from his back pocket. "Speaking of work ..." he says as he answers the call.

I should go. "Thanks for the tour," I say to Susanne as I retreat.

"Wait!" she calls out. "Let us give you some home-brewed Kombucha." She disappears inside for a moment, then returns with what appears to be a plastic Coca-Cola bottle.

"Kombucha?" I think that's what I screamed a few days ago in the campground shower when it suddenly turned icy-cold. I accept the small bottle of mystery liquid, wondering what it could possibly contain. It's a peculiar shade of dark green.

"It's great for your skin and helps with digestion and stress. Give it a try. Oh, and we don't need the bottle back as long as you promise to recycle it."

Kombucha. I wonder if it's also good for locating missing spouses or repairing a leaky radiator. I hold the bottle up to the light and shake it gently. "What's in it?"

"It's an ancient Chinese brew for good health. It's mostly green tea fermented with yeast and good bacteria."

That's probably an improvement over bad bacteria.

She continues, "We've also added blue-green algae for protein, improved memory, and increased energy. The taste takes a little getting used to."

I'll bet. "Thanks, Susanne. I'll save it for later." Probably much later, although I know I'll feel guilty if I don't at least take a sip.

I make my way back to my tiny cabin and borrowed car, load my sleeping gear and toiletries into the front passenger seat, and check my watch. I should be back in Salida well before noon. I consider calling the repair shop to make sure they're making progress, but decide to trust that things will go as planned for a change.

Waiting for a motorhome the size of a Greyhound Tour Bus to roll past, I follow it to the campground exit and watch for an opportunity to pass it once we're on the road.

The scenery seems more impressive this morning than it did when I drove over the high mountain pass last night. At its crest, no trees are growing and there are scattered patches of snow still clinging to the mountain slopes above me, despite the late July date. Rolling hills and rocky, jagged peaks spread out below, blankets of evergreens appearing several hundred feet below this lofty viewpoint, mountains taking on every hue of blue as my eyes follow the ranges into the distance. I roll down my window briefly and feel a chilly blast of air. As the road descends, the air seems to thicken and most definitely warms.

Arriving at the repair shop, I'm almost afraid to step inside. They promised to call me when my car was ready, but there's no notification on my phone of either a missed call or a voice message. Well, I might as well get this over with.

"Hi. I'm here for my Jeep Cherokee," I say as brightly as I can, hoping my cheerful tone will result in good news. Young Ron is behind the counter again.

"What's your name?" he says.

As I did yesterday, I give him my name and explain what's being done with my car. Again, he consults the computer, clicking and tapping enough keys that I begin to wonder if he's typing out the Gettysburg Address. "Okay," he says at last. "Yeah. It's almost ready."

I didn't realize I had been holding my breath. I let it out in a long, relieved sigh. Ron disappears through the door into the work area and I stand there, wondering if I should go sit down in what passes for a waiting area or remain here to await further news. As I glance outside, I almost cheer as I see my vehicle backing out of the service bays and being parked on the street.

Ten minutes and many dollars later, I'm on my way back to the serenity of Far Away Campground to enjoy my final two nights there before I decide where I want to go next.

Chapter 12

The campground is quiet this afternoon. As I drove in, I noticed that many of the vehicles that I've seen parked in front of their trailers or alongside the larger motorhomes are gone. I hope their owners are off having fun rather than making repeated trips to the nearest town for supplies and emergency repairs. The site next to mine which previously held a tent now features a tiny, bright yellow trailer which I remember Bob called a tear-drop, because of its shape. It's adorable, but I can't imagine there's room in it for anything beyond a bed. I probably have more headroom in the back of my Jeep.

After setting up my stove on the picnic table again and rearranging my sleeping area, I pull out my journal. The last time I wrote in it was the night the thieves broke into my car. Thank goodness I had it with me in my room – I'd be mortified if some punks got their hands on it and read it to each other for amusement!

Flipping it open to my final entry, I read:

> On to Colorado tomorrow – my adventure is finally beginning! I'm ready to start a new life and put all the bad stuff behind me.

Ha. Little did I know.

Flipping to the front pages, I skim through my comments.

> I keep racking my brain, trying to understand why he'd leave. Was it our disagreement about going to the Morgensterns for Thanksgiving? I told him we didn't have to go if he didn't want to. Even if it was that, how could something that minor cause him to leave and not even send me a note telling me what's wrong?!?

Several pages later, I wrote as if I were penning a letter to mail to Franklin:

> Please let me know where you are. This is simply cruel. How long did you plan this? Your old phone number is disconnected, your email address doesn't work, and now I find that your Social Security and pension deposits have stopped, so you must have changed those over to some new bank account.
> Why are you doing this??? What did I do to you to deserve this treatment???

I flip pages, my thoughts and emotions revealing themselves to me again like a time-lapse movie.

> It must be another woman. What else could it be? I thought his waning interest in sex was simply a part of growing older. But that sweet final night before he walked out – was that just his way of saying goodbye? This is killing me!

I sniff and wipe my eyes at this, my most precious yet painful memory. We both had tears in our eyes as we lay together – mine were tears of joy at his tenderness and loving attention. I had thought at the time that his tears were also for the warmth and devotion of our lovemaking. Now I still agonize over whether his were tears of regret for what he was about to do, or sorrow for what our bond *used* to mean to him.

Thumbing through the pages, weeks pass, then months. I mourn the loss of his companionship, then rage at his obvious lack of communication.

> How did I <u>not</u> know you were unhappy with our marriage? Why didn't you ever try to sit down and tell me what was bothering you? I had no idea something was wrong, right up to the moment you announced that you were leaving. How could you throw away 40 yrs of history like it meant nothing? Like <u>I</u> meant nothing? When did you become so cruel?

A lump forms in my throat. I shake it off. He's been gone nine months now, and he's not coming back. If a human being can develop from an egg and be born nine months later, then surely it's time for me to emerge from mourning and bitterness and move on.

"Hey, you're back! I thought you'd left without saying goodbye."

Swiftly closing my journal and stuffing it into my food box, I swipe my eyes then turn to face my visitor. "Hi, Bob. Yeah, I'm still around. I had some car trouble to take care of, but ... well, here I am."

Bob is wearing the same plaid shorts he had on a few days back, but fortunately his Hawaiian-patterned shirt hangs well below his gut. No bathrobe. His eyebrows dip low in the middle as he frowns. "You doing okay there, Ellie? Need any help with anything?"

I'm not sure if he picked up on my mood or is just playing the car-trouble, man-to-the-rescue card. Or both. "Everything's fine now. I had to replace the radiator."

He nods, his face relaxing. "Too bad – that had to cost a pretty penny. Well, good to see you're still around."

"For another couple of nights, anyway. How about you?"

He scratches his belly and squints up at the heavens, as if looking for a sign telling him what his travel plans should be. I follow his gaze and notice dark clouds blanketing the western sky. "Moving on sometime next week. I'm going to work my way over toward Winnemucca and go to Burning Man from there."

I've heard the name before, but the only thing I know about Burning Man is that a huge, man-shaped structure gets set on fire and there are enormous numbers of people attending, creating a temporary city in the middle of the desert for several days. I'm not someone who enjoys large gatherings, but apparently Bob is. "Sounds interesting," I say, wanting to be polite.

"No offense, Ellie, but I'm thinking it wouldn't be your sort of gig. Although that's kind of presumptuous of me to say so."

I smile and reassure him that he's probably correct. On that note, Bob waves and heads back toward his campsite.

***

Keeping an eye on the darkening clouds, I fire up my camp stove and begin heating water for cooking macaroni and cheese. As I wait for it to come to a boil, I chop up some fresh broccoli and add it to the water, waving away the mosquitoes that have started to circle. Thunder in the distance warns me to be prepared, so I pack up everything I don't need for the immediate task of preparing dinner and stow it in the back of the car. I stick my bowl and fork into the center console between the front seats. Returning to my stove, I pour dry noodles into the roiling water and start a timer on my phone just as the first few drops of rain splash onto my bare arm and into my hair. As I stir the pot and wait for it to boil again, several more drops strike. And more still. Scurrying back to my vehicle, I dig out the plastic sack that my new sleeping bag came in and drape it over my head before returning to my stove.

Stop raining, stop raining! But Mother Nature is doing exactly the opposite. Lightning flashes above me with a crash of thunder following only seconds later. Water is pouring down, splashing off the picnic table and battling the flame from the gas burner, which hisses like an angry cat before surrendering to the onslaught. I have the presence of mind to turn the burner dial to the "off" position before snatching the cooking pot from the stove and sloshing over to my car. The plastic bag falls to the soggy ground, but I manage to set the hot pot on the driver's seat, scurry back to retrieve the bag, dash around to the other side, and hop into the passenger seat, slamming the door behind me.

My hair is dripping into my face and my clothes cling to me. Miraculously, the pot of partially-cooked noodles and broccoli hasn't spilled, but I lift it off the fabric seat and check that it hasn't burned a hole in the upholstery. There's a noticeable damp circle there, but it appears to be all right, so I set the pot back down. My windows fog up while the loud drumming of the deluge outside continues.

Since the water is still very hot, the noodles should keep cooking for a bit if I just leave them be. Unfortunately, the outside temperature has dropped dramatically with the arrival of the rain, and even the interior of the car is becoming noticeably cooler. My arms are covered with goosebumps and I start to shiver, but all my extra clothes are in the very back of the Jeep and I don't want to step outside again.

I execute a complex series of moves to shift my bowl from the center console to the dash; hold the cooking pot level while I scoot my bottom half on the passenger seat, half on the console; set the pot down where my right buttock used to be as I continue scooting sideways; then finally untangle my legs and situate myself in the driver's seat; all without spilling boiling water on my lap!

My whole purpose for this agility test was so I could start the engine and turn on the heat, but all my gyrations have served to warm me back up. My phone alarm chimes, so I fish out a few noodles with my fork and test them. *Crunch*. I think I'd prefer eating the cardboard box they came in. I wipe a circle on the foggy window and squint out at the picnic table. Rats – that's what I was afraid of – I left the packet with the cheese sauce out in the rain.

For the next twenty minutes, I carefully retrieve every little chunk of blanched broccoli from the warm pot and munch slowly, staring at nothing and listening to the rain gradually diminish. The thunder and lightning retreat and everything is hushed, interrupted only by the irregular *pings* of infrequent drops splattering on the roof. Eventually, I ease open a door, feeling the cool rush of air, and hold out a hand before sliding out and standing alongside my car. Tiptoeing my way around puddles, I dance my way over to check my stove. Not surprisingly, the base is filled with water. I detach the propane canister, pour out the water, and balance the stove and its attached lid in an inverted triangle on the table to let it continue to drip out. The cheese sauce pouch goes in my trash bag.

Shivering again, I make a quick bathroom stop and climb into the back of my car just as it begins sprinkling. Barely past eight o'clock in the evening, and I'm pretty much stuck inside my Jeep for the duration.

Notes to self: Buy a raincoat. Umbrella. Mosquito repellent. A-frame camper.

Because I can picture people like Bob in his motorhome, or Cindy and Lynetta in their fancy camper van, or Mason and Janice in their practical trailer all retreating to their small but dry homes on wheels, cooking dinner with their heaters running, eating at their little dining room tables, and spending the evening dry and warm, curling up with a good book and a hot cup of cocoa, or playing scrabble, or watching a movie.

Chapter 13

I awaken to azure skies and the exuberant songs of birds. Water drops sparkle in the sunlight, making the trees surrounding my campsite shimmer and glow, a million miniature prisms blinking in a rainbow of colors. Steam rises from my table as the sunlight kisses the wet wood.

Stretching my arms above me as high as they'll go, I feel a satisfying stretch in my upper back and shoulders. My new sleeping pad will never take the place of a real bed, but it made a world of difference in my comfort. I slept well, as I often do when a steady rain offers its hypnotic rhythms on the roof. Apparently, even a car roof will do.

My stove sputters to life when I light it, quickly boiling off the remaining moisture in its base, and I find myself humming as I sip hot coffee and stir fresh blueberries into my steaming oatmeal. It's been fun fantasizing about traveling around in a camper, although in the clarity of morning I know it's nothing more than just that – a fantasy, a pipe dream.

Yet, once I've cleaned up after myself, I set off to circle through the camp and feel a smile building on my face as I approach Bob's site. As I'd hoped, he's settled into his camp chair beside his unit, flipping through a magazine and slurping something from a large mug.

"'Morning," I call out.

He sets down his mug. "Looks who's out for a walk so bright and early. How'd you hold up last night? I was hoping you didn't float away."

With a laugh, I say, "Almost, but I managed to survive. I can't say the same about my supper. I'm thinking of buying one of those beach umbrellas so I can keep my stove going next time."

He raises an eyebrow. "You should have come over here and stayed high and dry. Sorry you had to deal with cooking in the rain." He shakes his head and points next door where a couple of young men have lifted their tent in the air and are shaking it energetically. They've got clothes and a tarp strung up between two large trees. "Those boys made the mistake of setting up their tent in a low spot. Said they woke up during the night floating in a couple inches of water. They told me they moved the tent around one in the morning, but their bags and pads were too soaked to use. At least you had a spot all set up in your car where you can stretch out to sleep. Try to picture those two spending most of the night in that compact hybrid of theirs."

Both men are tall – over six feet, I'd guess. I'm not sure even I could stretch out flat in the back of their car, and I'm only five foot four.

"So, Bob, I've been thinking about that A-frame camper you were showing me." *Am I really saying this?* "Can I get those people's contact information from you?" *And then what, Ellie?* I mentally scold myself. *Pull the money out of thin air?*

Bob rocks back in his chair and hoists his body to a standing position. "I'm glad you're following up on this. You won't believe how much more enjoyable it is to have a home you can take with you." He retreats inside his unit and returns shortly with a business card and a small pad of paper in hand. "Larry and Jenny are good folks. Tell them 'hi' from Big Bob Langley when you talk to them." He begins copying information from the card onto a piece of paper, then pauses, tapping the pad with his pen. "Actually, why don't I give them a call myself. I'll let them know your situation, with losing your home to that hurricane and all. I'm sure they'll give you a great deal. Like I said, really nice folks. And," he says, leaning closer and lowering his voice, "like I told you, I'm pretty sure they're loaded. As in, money isn't really an issue. But really *nice* folks," he insists again. "Not the selfish kind of rich people."

"I appreciate this, Bob," I say, looking over the information he's written. "I'll give the Feddersons a call this afternoon." This is nuts. What am I doing? I don't want to deplete my IRA to buy a camper. I don't even know if I'll still like camping in another few weeks, much less doing it long-term.

"It's a great little starter for camping. You can't go wrong."

Thanking Bob again, I continue my circuit around the camp. Although I'm definitely ready to sit and rest when I finish the loop, I'm nowhere near as tired as I was the first day I walked it. Despite all my trips into town, I've been walking more each day than I have in ages. I ponder this briefly before recalling that Franklin and I used to take walks many mornings after our first cups of coffee, then return home for breakfast. Before that, back in the California hills, I met up weekly with my neighbors, Claire and Nan, to stroll around the various subdivisions near ours, checking out landscaping and gaping at homes high up the hillsides that none of us could ever afford. Tragically, many of those were the houses that were destroyed by the wildfires.

Since Franklin left, I've turned into a couch potato. Moving around again in the fresh, mountain air is starting to actually feel *good*. I fill my small water bottle from the spigot nearest to my camp and set out again, this time following a sign marking a 0.3 mile trail to a scenic overlook.

I walk along the path, using care when I come across muddy stretches or step on soggy, decaying leaves on the ground. My senses come alive with smells of both summer blossoms and wet leaves, fragrant pine needles and rich, earthy soil. I pause along the way to examine flowers of blue, yellow, white, and red and to search high in the tree tops for a bird or other small creature announcing my presence to the universe. Tired, but euphoric, I emerge into a clearing and inch forward onto a granite rock outcropping to gasp in awe at the panorama before and below me. Hills of a dozen shades of green roll away toward the horizon, with a shining, twisting river winding its way through the valley below. Farther away, mountains appear in hues of blue with a swash of white clouds distinguishing the peaks from the sky.

Carefully, I manage to lower myself to sit on an edge of rock, taking care to remain well back from the steep drop-off. I sip my water and try to take it all in, shading my eyes to watch a hawk floating at eye level, yet high above the valley, its raucous and haunting call being echoed by another bird in the distance.

I used to love coming to the mountains when I was growing up in Colorado. Franklin and I chose our dream location in a mountainous area of California, before disaster moved us in another direction. I've missed this sort of beauty. I should never have agreed to move back east, but my husband insisted that he wanted to return to *his* roots. Not having a clear idea of my own aside from leaving our damaged home, I acquiesced to his wishes, not realizing how much I felt like a square peg in a round hole in South Carolina. Or like a polar bear on Waikiki beach, as Franklin would say.

Now, my direction is entirely up to me. I just need to figure out where the hell I'm going.

Chapter 14

I admit it; I'm a coward.

When I returned to camp after my lovely hike yesterday, I couldn't bring myself to call the people about their A-frame camper. The news would be bad – I just knew it. The price would be much too high or they'd have already sold it and I'd be so disappointed, now that I've been foolish enough to allow myself to daydream about owning an adorable little trailer like that. Instead, I must remind myself to be realistic, to stop fantasizing about something that's unattainable. As I've done in the past, I'll keep repeating those messages until my brain convinces my heart to let go of the impossible and to come back down to earth.

I focus on the task at hand – spotting the turn-off for the camping area I hope to stay in for the next 3 nights. Intrigued by their Wildflower Festival, which I missed out on a week or so ago, I hoped I might still be able to view the colorful meadows surrounded by sheer, rocky peaks in the Crested Butte area. Unfortunately, plenty of other people must have had the same idea, since every campground with online reservations was already full by the time I was looking. Expanding my search radius, and spending time making numerous phone calls, I failed to find anything that could be reserved in advance. Finally, after asking me what type of vehicle I'm driving, a helpful gentleman gave me detailed directions to a dirt road with a number of spots where I can simply pull off the road and camp. "Bring all your own water and food," he instructed. "These are primitive spots."

After passing the tiny number sign for the County Road I'm supposed to take, I locate a place to turn around and give it another pass. I follow a gravel road for six miles, then turn again onto a much narrower dirt path. Averaging only about eight miles per hour, my Jeep bounces and lurches its way forward and I spot a camper mounted on a pickup truck parked in a small clearing beneath a copse of trees. This must be what the man was talking about as a primitive camping site. I continue past a pull-off which slants up a short rise, looking for a level spot where I can park. Someone has beat me to the next flat site, which looks ideal, but a few hundred feet beyond that is a setting that I like even better.

It's also on a bit of a rise, but it levels out at the top. Someone has crafted a short bench from tree stumps and a thick log, and I test it out. From my perch, I gaze south, where the trees open up, revealing a broad meadow of greens and brilliant yellows. Beyond, the high peaks in the distance display swashes of snow in their north-facing gullies.

I whisper aloud, This is perfect!

I take a few minutes to rearrange the scrambled items in the back of my Jeep. The one- and two-gallon water jugs tipped over part way during the bouncy ride, but didn't spill. My new four gallon container sits solidly in the very back of the car, wedged in place by my camp stove and tied to a hook in the ceiling. Later, I'll wriggle it closer to the back so I can fill my cooking pot from its built-in plastic spigot. But for now, I close and lock the car and set out to explore the scenery.

A very narrow path leads from my chosen spot out into the meadow. It steers me to a narrow creek which I'm able to cross by stepping onto a flat rock poking out of the water. On the other side, it splits and splits again, meandering into the high grasses and an ocean of chest-high flowers with petals like rays of sunshine. My breath catches with the beauty.

Eventually my legs grow tired and I make my way back to my campsite where I sit on the primitive bench for a while until my rear end begins to ache. It's about time to start dinner, so I lay my camp stove atop a flat rock and use the back of my vehicle to set up my miniature cutting board. After slicing up a potato, carrot, onion, and a bratwurst I bought on my way here, I return to my stove to cook it all up, my mouth watering as the ingredients start to sizzle.

I still have a bad habit of cooking far more than I can eat, despite cutting back considerably on quantities. Franklin's a big man with a huge appetite. The upside is that I can reheat my leftovers tomorrow and have a second meal. Sated and happy, I relax for a few minutes to let my dinner settle and to enjoy the dramatic lighting on the distant peaks as the sun drops lower.

My reverie is interrupted by the unmistakable high-pitched buzz of a mosquito circling my head. I rise to my feet, waving it away and realize I haven't thought out how to deal with washing my frying pan and bowl without any sort of sink or running water. After stowing tomorrow's meal in my cooler, I swirl a bit of water in the dirty pan and walk thirty feet or so away from my car and cooking area to fling the water and food particles into a bush, then resume my energetic waving and swatting to discourage the biting insects.

Maybe that wasn't a smart idea. I wonder if there are bears or coyotes or other animals around who might be drawn to my camp if I throw smelly food about? Noting that there are still plenty of bits of onion and sausage stuck to the pan, I fetch some paper towels, dampen them, and do my best to wipe up the remaining food from both my bowl and the pan. That's better, but still greasy. I add a couple of drops of dishwashing liquid to the frying pan, heat up water in a pot, and pour it into the pan, scrubbing with a clean paper towel. The rinsing process requires several refills and I heat up even more of my limited water supply, tossing each batch of rinse water far from camp.

At this rate, my water supply is not going to last. I decide to ignore the grease in the future and simply wipe out my food as best I can, skip the soap, and swish a little boiling water over anything I've used.

Collecting up my soggy, food-laden paper towels, I stash them in an empty grocery bag which I stow on the floor of the car. The light is starting to fade and my bladder is feeling nature's call. Is there an outhouse around here? I didn't notice one when I drove in, so I set out on a short recognizance mission along the rough road, searching for one. Not willing to roam too far from my camp in the dimming light and becoming more uncomfortable, I return to my "home" and find a place to squat where I'm well-hidden by the trees. Not that I've seen anyone else driving or walking around for the past couple of hours. I return to the car and continue my preparations for the evening. Simple, everyday tasks now require thought and a little ingenuity – washing my face, brushing my teeth and rinsing – again, I fret about critters being attracted to the minty foam, so I do my spitting well away from the Jeep.

Ready to settle in to read for a bit before going to sleep, I turn my gaze upward and I'm astounded by the sparkling array of stars visible in the swatch of sky framed by the trees surrounding my little paradise. The milky way arcs across the sky like a rainbow of galaxies and the solid, reddish light of a brilliant planet glows like a beacon amidst the twinkling of its neighbors. An owl hoots nearby, and the gentlest of breezes brushes its cool fingers across my face. Instead of crawling into my car, I pull out my sleeping pad and lie on the ground where I have a clear view of the magnificent spectacle above me. Not until I begin to feel a slight chill do I awkwardly roll onto my knees and work my stiff body into a standing position.

Once cocooned inside my sleeping bag, I peer out my car window until I spot the streak of a shooting star. *Goodnight,* I whisper, and close my eyes.

Chapter 15

I've spent a delightful morning browsing through the shops and galleries in the quaint town of Crested Butte. Following a relaxing lunch seated outside a small café, marveling at the majesty of the peak by the same name, I set out to explore the roads leading higher into the mountains. Following a series of well-maintained gravel roads, I explore the scenery, stopping often to examine the ever-changing array of flowers and trees as the road climbs above 10,000 feet, then loops back down to the town a thousand feet lower.

My final stop is at the local library, where I set up my laptop and browse listings of small campers for sale. Calling up my cash flow spreadsheet, I play with a dozen scenarios, trying to find a way to afford even an older unit without tapping into my IRA. Although I've become a bit more competent at camping over the past few weeks, I can't picture myself living out of my Jeep terribly much longer. I love being outdoors, but need just a few comforts of home as well.

If I knew where I'd like to settle long-term, I could rent a place. At this point in my journey, I don't feel remotely close to making that decision. Either a budget motel or an extended stay hotel might be a possibility, but when I read through the reviews of the affordable ones in the towns and cities where I might be willing to spend a month or more, I quickly eliminate that idea. If only someone would just *give* me a camper as a gift! If I had that covered, I'm sure I could make my monthly budget work.

Damn you, Franklin. We had it all planned out, living off his annuity and Social Security while I took the occasional proofreading project. Once I turn sixty-six, we figured I could stop working since we'd be drawing from my Social Security as well and we could also tap into my IRA. When I first discovered that he left me exactly half of our joint checking and savings balances and had pre-paid our rent for half a year, I was relieved that he had at least played fair in that respect. But now that I've had plenty of time to think about it, and realize that I was barely able to afford the rent on our apartment once that fell back into my lap, I recognize that he left me in a real bind. If I start taking my Social Security in another year when I turn sixty-two – the earliest I can begin – I'll be drawing a lower amount for the rest of my life. Meanwhile, he's got all his retirement income flowing in, and a far greater pool of funds to draw from than mine.

I close down my computer and return to my car, driving slowly back toward my backcountry campsite and forcing thoughts of money and missing husbands from my mind. By the time I park in my lovely spot again, I feel like my personal storm clouds have dissipated. I continue to unwind, immersed in my view of the flower-filled meadow and the distant peaks, watching breathlessly as a herd of thirty or more elk ramble through the valley less than a football field length away.

My dinner is simple tonight, since I brought back a "doggie bag" of leftovers from my generous-sized lunch. No pots or pans to clean. I settle on my log bench to enjoy the fiery colors of the clouds over the peaks on the horizon as the cool evening nestles in. The bug repellent I've doused myself with seems to be working, as mosquitoes approach but retreat in disgust. The colors shift and fade until I spot the first bright star of the night.

A scuffling sound behind me causes me to spin around quickly, a chill rising up my spine. Just beyond my car, I spot a large, dark figure. A bear? A man?

I choke out a loud but hoarse, "Hello?" and jump to my feet, wishing there was more between me and the unidentifiable form than just the low log bench. If I run to my car, can I possibly get inside and lock the doors before he – or it – can reach me? I shift my weight slightly in the direction of my Jeep and the dying light reflects in my visitor's eyes for an instant.

I freeze, terrified to move again and still trying to determine what I'm seeing, my heart pounding so violently that I wonder if I'll die from a heart attack before the *thing* can harm me. After what feels like an eternity, the intruder changes position. I clasp both hands over my thumping chest, laughing like a mad woman. As it turns sideways and walks slowly away from my camp, even in the dim light I recognize the graceful gait of a mule deer. Facing me straight on, she presented a completely different silhouette. I was nearly scared to death by Bambi.

Nonetheless, I climb into my vehicle and lock the doors immediately. What if it *had* been a bear? Or a stranger who might do me harm? My idyllic campsite no longer feels like the safe paradise I thought it was, although I recognize that it's only my perspective that has changed, not the setting.

I think I'll stick to camping where there are other people around from now on.

Lying in my bag, I decide to take a small step toward what I'm coming to realize is my dream. In the morning, I'll follow up on the A-frame camper Bob told me about. Maybe nothing will come of it, but it can't hurt to at least make a phone call.

***

"Yes, of course. Bob told us to expect your call, Ellie. He's a delightful character, isn't he?"

Jenny Fedderson has a warm, enthusiastic voice on the phone. We make small talk for a few minutes before I bring us back to the reason I called. "Do you still have that camper for sale?" I literally cross my fingers.

"We certainly do. We've had a couple of inquiries about it, but no one's actually come to see it yet, so we're thinking they might just be lookie-loos. Bob told us about your situation, fleeing your home with that hurricane bearing down on you. That must have been terrifying!"

"Actually, with all the warnings, I left well before it came ashore. But it has been difficult, and I have no desire to be in that sort of situation again."

"No, I would think not. So, now you're looking for a camper to live in until you settle down again?"

Okay, here goes. "That's my dream, but my reality is that I'm on a tight budget, so I don't know if I can afford the sort of unit I'd really like."

"And what sort of unit would that be?" she asks.

"Well, if I had unlimited resources, maybe something like Bob has," I say. "No, I take that back. I can't imagine myself driving something that size. I've thought about a camper van, but the nice ones seem extremely pricey. So, I think a camp trailer would suit me the best. So," I take a deep breath and ask the big question, "how much are you asking?"

She doesn't say anything for a beat or two. Listening closely, I think I hear muffled voices on the line. Perhaps she and her husband are conferring. I cross another pair of fingers. Finally, she replies with a number that's lower than I had expected based on my research, but still a significant stretch for me to afford.

"Would you like to come see it?" she asks. "We're in Denver."

I must be nuts, but I say yes. Denver is only about a half day's drive, but it's already late morning and I don't want to arrive close to rush hour. "Would tomorrow work for you?" I ask.

Jenny and I work out the timing and I enter their address into my phone to make sure it can help me navigate to their house. "I really appreciate this," I say.

"Our pleasure. Larry and I are looking forward to meeting you. See you soon."

I slump back in my car seat and shake my head while grinning like a buffoon. My husband always told me I needed to be more spontaneous. Well, what do you think of me now, Franklin?!

You need a camper like a Chihuahua needs a curling iron.

Screw you, Franklin.

Chapter 16

While my previous campsite seemed too isolated, the commercial one I landed in about ninety minutes outside of Denver felt like parking in the lot of a Walmart Supercenter during the height of a Black Friday sales event. My vehicle was penned in by two mega-monster motorhomes, both with slide-outs that encroached on my picnic table on one side and my passenger-side door on the other. With their windows hovering over me, allowing a direct view of my sleeping area, I did my best to hang articles of clothing from my Jeep's windows for a semblance of privacy. I had also forgotten how much warmer it would be once I dropped down to the east side of the Rockies. For the first few hours in my claustrophobic parking spot, I roasted inside my car.

I'd love to sleep in, now that it's cool and the sun isn't quite up, but someone nearby has been opening and closing their car doors repeatedly for the past ten minutes. Slam. Slam-slam. Then a long pause and slam-slam-slam. Pause. Slam.

"Just leave the damn doors open," I moan. Slam. The loud roar of an engine starting is accompanied by a deep-pitched rumble, and after a minute or so I hear what sounds like an eighteen-wheeler drive slowly past, the gravel roadway crunching under its tires. Wide awake, I decide to arise.

As I sip a hot cup of coffee and munch on a donut, all compliments of the commercial campground, I feel my excitement and anticipation build for my visit to Denver late this morning. When I check my email and find an inquiry from an author who's been one of my clients in the past, it feels like a good omen. I put together a proposal and fire it back to her. If she gives me the green light, this job would bring in enough to pay for a month of camping if I shop around for a good rate.

***

The Feddersons live in an upscale neighborhood, dotted with McMansions surrounded by immaculate landscaping but lacking old, established trees. Spotting the distinctive "A" shape of the camper I've come to see makes it simple to locate the right address.

I park on the street and try to tamp down my enthusiasm before emerging from my car. Walking slowly up the driveway toward the trailer, I spot the upper reaches of a tall motorhome parked beyond a six-foot privacy gate alongside the house.

"Hello!" A neatly-dressed woman of around seventy or so steps out the front door of the house, followed closely by a man I'm assuming is her husband. She waves enthusiastically as she approaches. "You must be Ellie. I'm Jenny and this is Larry."

"And this," Larry says, sweeping his arm in the direction of the camper, "is Little Roamer. That," he adds, pointing to the gleaming RV behind the gate, "is The Fedderhouse."

"Clever names," I say, already trying out 'Little Roamer' in my mind to see if I like it or might come up with something else.

"See, the model is called an A-Roamer, so it seemed natural to name our baby Little Roamer," Jenny explains. They both seem so earnest, like they're talking about a beloved pet.

Larry gestures for me to step inside and perches on the step describing Little Roamer's many features as I take it all in. It's similar to the A-frame camper I visited last week, but now that I'm considering owning one, I try to take in everything. Larry gladly describes every switch and knob, encourages me to peek inside cabinets, and joins me inside to demonstrate how to convert the queen-sized bed to a couch of sorts and how to create another sleeping area where the dining table usually resides.

"We've made some changes to suit our lifestyle," Jenny says, squeezing inside as well. Larry sits at the table so we can still move around. "Unless you don't want them, we're including the plastic boxes for storing food or organizing your clothes. And we added the foam mattress topper for the big bed. You can have the sheet set as well, since I modified a standard set so they'd fit the three inch mattress." She slides the bed back out and pats it. "It's so much more comfortable with the topper. Give it a try."

"Oh, no, I couldn't ..."

"Please! You've come all this way. Getting a good night's sleep is so important – of course you should try out the bed!"

Feeling somewhat sheepish, I slip off my shoes and ease myself into a supine position. It takes a conscious effort not to moan with pleasure as my back muscles relax into the mattress. I feel like Goldilocks when she discovered the bed that felt just right.

I overcome my body's reluctance to leave this marvelous spot and we continue the tour by circling the outside of the camper and again discussing every hose and cubbyhole and plug. I try to memorize everything, but don't completely understand what some of the features actually do.

We conclude with the two of them demonstrating how to fold the camper's walls down and how to set it back up again. "It's like one of those transformer toys," I say, delighted at how simple yet dramatic the change is. "But, I don't know if I'm strong enough to raise the sides by myself."

They insist I give it a try. The first time, I struggle to lift a wall that forms part of the "A" shape, but after Larry has me step up on a small stool and position myself for a better angle, I succeed. We repeat the process twice more, setting up and locking the walls in place, then releasing the locks and folding the sides down.

"What do you think?" Larry asks.

Jenny smiles and nods. "I can tell you really like Little Roamer."

I've been picturing myself living out of this adorable camper. Inside, the large windows offer views in every direction, giving me a sense of still being outdoors but with screened windows to keep out the mosquitoes and a door that can be locked. There are cushioned seats and overhead lights, tiny yet practical kitchen appliances. Hot running water in a little sink. And a bed that's every bit as comfortable as anything I've slept in.

"I do like it. And the price you're asking is more than fair. But I just don't know if I can afford to come up with the full amount. I'm sorry."

They exchange glances and some message passes between them.

Jenny places a hand on my shoulder in a comforting sort of way. "Ellie, based on our phone conversation, we thought that might be your answer. Look, like I said, Bob explained about how you had to leave your home because of the hurricane. Now, I like to think I'm a pretty good judge of character."

"We both are," Larry says.

"And Bob makes three. I don't think you're someone who would try to pull the wool over anyone's eyes about your situation."

"No, absolutely not. The thing is, the housing disaster back where I was living is going to be a mess for quite a while, and I have no desire to move back there even when things improve. To be honest, I've had several major disruptions in my life over the past few years, and I'm trying to reinvent myself, so to speak. But I don't know yet what that's going to entail. I'm kind of flying by the seat of my pants right now."

"So, here's what we're thinking," Larry says, looking at his wife as he speaks. "What could you afford as a down payment?"

"A down payment? You mean, take out a loan for the rest? But, I don't have anything other than my Jeep to use as collateral, and it's ten years old."

"We'd be fine with just your word as collateral," Jenny says, smiling.

"Oh, no. You don't even know me. That's too much to ask."

Larry crosses his arms over his chest and shakes his head. "I didn't hear Ellie ask, did you?"

"No. Definitely not," Jenny replies.

He continues. "Nope. All I heard was my wife telling you what we're comfortable with. Now, let me repeat my question. How much can you afford to put down?"

Tears fill my eyes as I begin to realize that they're serious. I have just over $6,000 left in my savings right now and another $1,500 in checking. Pulling $6,000 from my IRA to replenish my savings isn't going to kill me. I'll take on more work. Start drawing Social Security next year. Although I still don't know where I want to eventually land, I feel in my gut that living out of this little camper is what I should do for now. Maybe for a number of years. Dabbing my eyes, I offer the $6,000 as a down payment.

Within minutes, we've settled on a payment plan for the balance. Jenny and I sit at a table in a decorative gazebo in their yard and sip lemonade while Larry disappears into the house for a short while. When he returns, we sign the agreement that he's printed out. Calling my bank, I arrange to pick up a cashier's check at a local branch today and I use an app on my phone to transfer funds from my IRA to my checking to replenish what I'm spending.

With plans to return after lunch to finalize everything, I run my errands but find I'm too excited to eat. After confirming for the tenth time that the cashier's check is still safely tucked into a zipped pocket in my purse, I drive around for another half hour before returning to the Fedderson's at our agreed-upon time.

Their generosity continues as they provide me with an assortment of gadgets and hardware to properly hook up the trailer to my Jeep, secure it for towing, and lock it up when it's parked.

"Thank goodness your Cherokee already has a tow package with a brake controller!" Larry says, poking his head under my steering column. I had no idea what that device did. It was there when we bought the two-year-old Jeep.

With plenty of coaching and the assistance of my car's back-up camera, we hitch the trailer to my vehicle and I practice setting up the safety chains and everything else that needs to be plugged in or clipped on. Finally, loaded down with manuals and a plastic bag filled with homemade peanut butter cookies, I roll slowly down their driveway, checking my rearview mirror every few seconds to confirm that the trailer is still following me.

"Thank you again!" I call out my window before driving away with my new home.

Little Roamer, my running-away-from-home home.

Chapter 17

Following the Fedderson's advice, I opt to spend my first night in my new camper at a large RV campground whose online reviews raved about the "level sites" and "helpful staff." After registering at the office, I'm escorted by a man riding a golf cart to my campsite, where he even shows me exactly how far to pull forward to be able to connect easily to the water and power supplies. As promised, when I check the level side-to-side, my unit is perfectly balanced. I choose to leave the trailer hitched to my car, and find I'm able to jack up the trailer tongue as well as the back end of my SUV to a level position front-to-back. No muss, no fuss.

It only takes me two tries to lift the large A-frame walls into place, flip up the triangle walls, and lock everything in place. Including the time I spent talking myself through each step, the whole process lasted a mere fifteen minutes. With practice, I can imagine getting it done in less than two.

Although the weather is perfectly cooperative for cooking outdoors, I prepare my ravioli dinner on the gas stove inside my darling camper. With all the curtains tied back and every window opened to its fullest, I also eat inside at the little table, able to observe the happenings surrounding me in every direction as I dine. My cheeks are aching from all my smiling! Even washing my dishes is a simple task, although

I puzzled over where to dump the dirty water that emptied from my sink into a large bucket the Feddersons provided. "You don't have a gray water tank. Use the bucket and empty it manually into the drainpipe before it overflows," they told me. It takes me a few minutes to locate the drain they described, but now I know what to look for.

My first night in my camper is a delight. The curtains darken my sleeping area, a vent in the roof lets in fresh air, and the foam mattress is as comfortable as any bed I've slept in. In the morning, following a relaxed breakfast, I discover that folding down the walls and locking everything up is even faster and simpler than setting up was. Carefully, I review the checklist Larry and Jenny gave me for preparing to travel and give my folded trailer a pat of congratulations. We're ready to roll!

***

I'm starting to tune out the annoyed drivers who fly past me, some laying on the horn and others actually flipping me the bird. Nobody is more aware than I am that I'm only driving 50 in a 65 zone. Sorry, folks. I'm pretty freaked out dragging this camper down the highway, so I'm staying in the right lane and working hard to keep my foot off the brake and my eyes off the rear-view mirror, where all I can see is my new baby and the top-most portion of a tractor-trailer following a few hundred yards behind me. So far, my trailer hasn't fallen off.

As the miles pile up, I gain a bit more confidence and speed up to 55. But after I top out on a high pass through the mountains and start downhill, I shift down to avoid riding my brakes and the brakes on the trailer. Huge trucks pass me on the winding highway as I reclaim my title as slowest moving vehicle.

When I finally reach flatter territory, I feel like I've just run a marathon. Spotting a generously-sized and paved pull-off, I escape the traffic and stop, turning off the engine and resting my forehead on the top of my steering wheel.

"Ma'am? Are you okay?"

I jerk to an upright position with a gasp. A State Patrol officer peers at me through the driver's side window and gestures for me to roll it down.

"Ma'am, is everything all right?"

"Oh, I'm so sorry, officer. I was just resting. This is my first day pulling a trailer on mountain roads and I found it rather stressful," I say, hoping I'm not going to get a ticket for driving too slowly or for breaking some unknown rule about hauling a trailer along a highway. "I'm feeling fine now." I hope my smile looks like a woman who truly is *fine* rather than one who is too frazzled to be trusted behind a wheel.

He seems to study me for a minute, then leans in slightly and lets his eyes explore the interior of my SUV. Apparently satisfied that I didn't suffer a heart attack, nor am I being forced to drive to the Western Slope by an escaped murderer hiding in my back seat, he gives my car door a few encouraging pats, reminds me to drive safely, and returns to his cruiser. With a long exhale, I close my eyes for a moment, but open them again in case he can see my face in my side mirror. I check it to see if he is leaving yet. Nope. After a minute, I realize he's probably waiting for me to demonstrate my ability to merge back onto the highway, so I watch until I can't see a single vehicle in my side-view mirror, then pull out and resume my journey. In my right-side mirror, I see him follow me out of the pull-out and hope he'll soon pass me, since he disappears from view when he's directly behind my trailer. Several slow miles later, he pulls into the left lane and accelerates past. I continue plodding along at 55, relieved that he's turned his attention to other traffic.

By late afternoon, I've begun relaxing enough to occasionally be aware of the scenery around me rather than focusing one hundred percent of my attention to scanning the road ahead and all of my mirrors. Passing through deep valleys, the sparkling reflection of sunshine in a stream beside the highway catches my eye. The aspen trees seem to shimmer in the late afternoon light, with just a hint of autumn gold starting to appear amidst the sweeping swatches of bright kelly green leaves painting the sides of the mountains.

I'll be staying a week at my next campsite, giving me time to explore the Four Corners region, sampling the beauty and history of intersecting borders of Colorado, New Mexico, Arizona, and Utah. Ancient cliff dwellings, natural towers and monoliths of red rock, craft shops, and wineries fill my list of places to visit.

Unlike last night, my campsite tilts slightly to one side. The left side is lower, I decide after studying the bubble in the level on the front of the trailer. Reviewing Larry's instructions in my mind, I set up several of the hard plastic tiles he gave me directly behind the left trailer tire and carefully ease the vehicles backwards so the tire rolls up on top of the little orange pile of blocks, which interlock almost like Lego toys.

I know before I even step out of the car that I backed up too far and rolled off the back side of my pile. This time, I pull forward ever so slowly – success! Or maybe not. Checking the level, I discover that I've made things much worse. I climb back into the car, roll the trailer off the blocks, move the blocks to the opposite side, and try again.

Success? I pump my fist in celebration – the trailer is level!

Next, I use the trailer jack to raise the front of the unit until that direction, too, is level. Except the trailer is still attached to the hitch, so I haven't freed my Jeep from the trailer yet. Okay, I've got this. For the next five minutes or so, I attempt to get the hitch ball to drop out of the coupler, but no matter what I do, vehicle and trailer stay connected. I flip the locking lever back into its locked position then open it again. I try jacking the trailer up, hoping gravity will help, but all I accomplish is lifting the back of my car. Frustrated, I walk back to the registration office and beg for help.

Alice, the park employee who comes to my rescue, takes one look at the hitch and grasps the locking lever, giving it a sharp tug. "It needs to be all the way back like this," she says as she rapidly spins the crank on the jack until the hitch pops free from the coupler.

I'm about to thank her when I realize the trailer is rolling backwards off the leveling blocks. "Help!" I scream, but Alice has already grabbed a handle on the front of the trailer and is pulling with all her might.

"Block the wheels!" she shouts. "Where are your chocks?"

Damn! Larry told me to always be sure the wheels couldn't move *before* unhooking. So many steps to remember!

Reaching into the back of my car, I clutch four plastic chocks and scurry to wedge them in front and back of both trailer tires.

"So, that's a step you always want to do before unhitching," Alice says, releasing her grasp on the trailer handle. "Good thing your site is nearly level and your camper is so lightweight. You don't want to try that maneuver with a thirty-six-footer."

"I'm so sorry." God, how embarrassing.

She waves me off. "Not a problem. I'll bet you won't ever forget those chocks again. Now, do you need any help hitching her back up and re-leveling?"

Oh, right. I've got to get the wheel back up on the orange blocks again. "No, that's okay. The only way I'm going to learn is to practice."

Nodding, she heads back to the office, but calls out, "Don't hesitate to let me know if you need anything else."

"Will do. Thanks again." Well, that should make for an entertaining story for the campground staff.

Before I begin the whole process again, I dig out the list of steps for setting up camp that Jenny Fedderson gave me. I was such a dunce to not refer to it in the first place. Reviewing it carefully, I draw a large star beside the note to always secure the wheels before unhitching. I annotate the list with a note about the hitch locking lever and promise myself to follow every step they've documented.

An hour after pulling into my site, the camper is fully set up independent of my Jeep, it is level and stabilized, I'm hooked up to water and electricity, and life is good. My goal is to knock my setup time down to five minutes, which the Feddersons promised was all it would take once I got past the learning curve.

But for now, I'm going to take a nap.

Chapter 18

It's not been quite a month since I fled the hurricane, and already I feel the desolate vacuum of my social life. I'm alone. Not that I was Ms. Social Butterfly while we lived in South Carolina, but I did have people to talk to on a regular basis. The ladies in my book club were always cordial and interested in a wide range of topics, although I wouldn't count any of them as close friends. Matthew, who volunteered on Tuesdays with me at the Botanic Gardens, seemed to relate to me as a surrogate aunt whom he could talk to about anything. We'd discuss his parents' chilly reaction when he dropped out of college to pursue a career as a sound technician, how to start a conversation with his girlfriend about their disagreements related to money, pros and cons of finishing his degree. Now that I think about it, we kept to our age-driven roles all the time. Never did he ask nor I offer personal details about my own life.

Of course, until last November, I always had my best friend and life partner to talk to, to share new experiences, reveal my joys and sorrows. Until he pulled his Disappearing Act.

Unable to think of a single other soul I'd feel comfortable calling up out of the blue, I make do with contacting my brother-in-law.

"Still AWOL, I assume." Franklin's departure is still our first topic of conversation whenever we talk.

Hank doesn't sound as shocked by my story of buying the camper/trailer as I expected. "Ellie, I must say I didn't think you'd take a step like that, but I'm happy for you. Cheryl and I love our motorhome, although we don't seem to get out as much as we imagined we would when we traded up to it. Maybe we can meet somewhere when you come back east."

With my only plan being to explore the western part of the country, I opt for a polite answer. "Yes, maybe we can."

I ramble for a while about the wonderful places I've visited, the dramatic views and glimpses of long-ago native civilizations, but sense that Hank is waiting for an opening to end the conversation. "Anyway," I say, "that's what I've been up to. I'm heading to the Flagstaff area next week where I'm staying at a campground for a full month."

"Can I send your mail there? You've got a fat packet that looks like something to do with your insurance." I hear him flipping through some papers. "A letter from United Way, an AARP magazine, Golf Now magazine, and the rest I'd consider to be junk."

Until I settle down somewhere, I'm having all my South Carolina mail forwarded to Hank's address. This is the first time he's received anything that I think warrants sending on. I provide him with the Flagstaff campground address and make a mental note to call them to let them know to expect his package. "Just send the insurance packet and the AARP magazine," I tell him. Hopefully, Franklin's golf magazine subscription will finally expire this month and that regular reminder of his absence will end. I consider suggesting that Hank tear it in shreds before tossing it into his recycling bin, but decide not to reveal my own ritual to him.

Tonight, I choose to sit outside to eat my dinner. I make a point of smiling and waving at every passerby, my camping neighbors out for a stroll around the loops. Nearly everyone returns my greeting, but nobody seems inclined to stop and introduce themselves. Once I clean up my kitchen, I set out to cruise the campground, longing for some human interaction.

I endure another of my heart-stopping, husky-man-with-white-hair moments when I spot a man seated outside an expansive motorhome. Silently, I scold myself for my gut reaction that is in total disagreement with my conscious determination to put my life with Franklin aside and move on. To teach my subconscious a lesson, I step to the edge of his site. "Beautiful unit you have there."

The man twists around in his chair to speak to me and I almost laugh out loud when I realize he's African American, probably in his 80s, and sports a beard and mustache. So much for resembling my missing husband. "Thank you. My wife and I have been full-timers for ten years now. We call her the 'Russell Road House'," he says, pointing to those very words painted above the door. Grasping the arms of his chair, he pushes himself to his feet and offers his hand to shake. "Bernie Russell," he says as a woman appears at the door to their camper and steps carefully down the stairs. "And this is my wife, Annie."

Annie's smile is warm and welcoming. "How're you doing? Where are you camped?" she asks after shaking my hand.

I introduce myself and point to the gap between a moderate-sized camper and a small motorhome. "You can't quite see it from here," I say. "It's small, but I think it works for me. I'm pretty new at camping," I admit.

"You have any questions or need help with something, don't you hesitate to ask," Bernie says.

Annie unfolds another camp chair. "Come sit. I just pulled some cookies from the oven. Would you like coffee?"

The old me would have politely declined her offer, but the new and lonely me is thrilled at the invitation. "Can I help you with that?" I ask.

She waves me off. "You just relax. Bernie, see if Ellie knows about how to get discounts and where to buy propane." She disappears into their unit.

For the next hour or so, we share stories. The Russells are working their way east, so I'm able to provide them with some interesting destinations around the region where I last lived, but mostly I prompt them for recommendations in the Northwest, Nevada, Utah, and Arizona, following their meandering path over the past several years. Annie jots down names of favorite places as Bernie prompts her. "Don't leave out Boyce Thompson Arboretum!" he says, waving his finger toward her list. Turning to me, he adds, "You'll want to allow at least half a day there. I'm sure you've never seen anything like it, and with your interest in plants ... Oh!" Pointing at his wife again, "Write down Organ Pipe Cactus National Monument and Kitt Peak near Tucson."

"Slow down, Bernie. I'm not writing this in shorthand, you know." Annie snickers as she scribbles furiously. "Don't forget that funky little rock shop we visited after Kitt Peak. What was its name?"

By the time I excuse myself, I'm holding a three-page list of recommendations of places to eat, walk, shop, learn, relax, and camp. At the rate they were coming up with ideas, I think they could have written a 300 page travel guidebook right there on the spot, if only Annie could keep up with Bernie's enthusiastic output. We promise to keep in touch by email.

There are periods when I question my impetuous decisions to buy the camper and take my time before settling down in one place. Maybe I should take root somewhere and find a full-time writing or editing position. Act my age. Yet, days like today when I marvel at the ingenuity and diverse building skills of Ancestral Puebloans, make a couple of new friends, and realize how much more fit and strong I feel than a month ago when I fled my apartment, I believe this strange journey may mark a turning point, my great escape from all the bad luck.

Chapter 19

As I drive toward Flagstaff, the landscape begins a remarkable transition. From broad, flat and barren desert, the land begins to undulate and rise in altitude. Scattered shrubs dot the land, growing more densely the higher I climb. Piñon pines and junipers rise above the prairie grasses and rabbit brush, then I spot the first tall evergreens. Ahead, on the horizon, a pair of majestic mountains grow ever taller as I approach, with the highway ahead seeming to climb to a pass between them. And now, gaining elevation on a long hill, the road is lined with a dense forest of stately Ponderosa pines.

My home base for the next thirty days is a small Ma-and-Pa campground called R-D RV Park. Rosie – the "R" in the facility's name – checks me in, handing me a packet of information about restaurants, shopping, hiking, and other attractions in the area. "As I told you when you called," she says, "R-D is for adults over 50 only. Now, if you have children or grandchildren coming to visit, they can park out front and walk back to your site, but they can't stay overnight."

"I don't expect any visitors," I say, leafing through the brochures and fliers.

She nods, picking up a walkie-talkie. "Danny, I need you to take a guest to 16."

I climb back into my vehicle as Danny arrives in a golf cart. Instead of leading me to the site, however, he pulls up next to my car door.

"I always like to ask this," he says, "so don't take offense or think I'm making any assumptions. But, how comfortable are you with backing into a site?"

My eyes open wide as it registers that I may have to actually back up my trailer more than a couple of feet to balance it. "I've never tried. I watched some online videos, but ..."

He gives me a reassuring smile. "Not to worry. I'll guide you through it every inch of the way."

Before I can beg him to simply take over the task entirely, he's rolling away in the cart, obviously expecting me to follow.

Danny is true to his word. Once he's led me to the precise spot he's chosen in the roadway, he walks alongside my window, coaching me to "turn your wheel right, now straighten, now right again, that's perfect, now harder to the right, good, and back to the left just a bit. Keep going, keep going, and stop."

We did it! My trailer is nestled in a space lined with Ponderosas and flowering bushes. Danny offers to help me hook up to the water and electricity, but those, at least, I know how to do. "Thank you so much!" I call out as he zips away.

Before I start, I read through my set-up checklist. Feeling more confident with each repetition, I work through the steps to level and block the trailer, unhook from the car, and raise the panels of the camper. Trying out an idea I had to move my stepstool slightly closer to the center of the trailer's length, I'm pleased to discover that the angle is an improvement, making it easier to raise the large sides into place, forming the "A" structure of the roof. I climb inside to lift the smaller triangle walls. This process still delights me – turning the squat, folded trailer into a tiny A-frame home.

I turn and push the second triangle into position and flip the two latches to lock it in place. Just as I reach down to pick up my box of food supplies, *bam*! I cry out in pain as I'm struck hard on the back of my head and my upper spine and I find myself sprawled atop my storage boxes after scraping a shin and banging a knee on the floor.

My eyes fill with tears, both from pain and frustration. I can't do this. Everything I try goes wrong.

Awkwardly, I manage to reposition myself so the edge of a box isn't poking me in the ribs. Looking up, I realize what just happened. A foot above my head is the first triangle wall I set up, now resting in a horizontal position. I must have forgotten to latch it in place. It stayed put briefly, then dropped on my head.

Moaning, I try to find purchase with my hands so I can scoot toward the center of the floor and stand up to attempt to raise the wall back to vertical. Everything hurts.

"Are you okay?" A woman's voice calls to me and I turn to see a head poking in the door just above floor level.

"I think so," I answer, but I can hear the tremor in my voice as a tear rolls down my face.

Within seconds, she's climbed inside and lifted the triangle wall, latching it on one end before kneeling over me. "Where are you hurt, dear? Can you stand?"

My mind sends me back to my eleven-year-old self, huddling in a makeshift cave of blankets and sheets draped over our seldom-used ping pong table in the basement of our house. My mother followed me to my favorite hidey-hole after I dashed into the house in tears after school.

"What happened, dear?" she asked as she crawled inside my little shelter with me.

That was the day Tonya West handed out invitations to her birthday party in the lunchroom cafeteria. Every girl at our table received one, except for me. As she distributed the last one from her stack, she looked directly at me and announced with a cruel smirk on her face, "Okay, that's everyone. Oh, sorry Ellie. We don't have enough room for you." As I fought off tears, everyone giggled. Gathering my tray, I hurried to my feet, anxious to make my escape. Somebody flung chocolate milk at me and I felt it soak through my blouse – I couldn't see who did it through my tears.

Mom stayed with me under that table for hours, comforting me and promising things would get better. She encouraged me to seek out some of the girls in my class who weren't part of that "cool girls" circle.

I hadn't thought of that incident in years.

My current rescuer offers me a hand, and helps me to my feet, then leads me to sit on a cushioned bench. I fetch a tissue from my pocket, blow my nose, and dry my eyes.

I'm a bit surprised now that I'm getting a good look at the lady. With her agility and strength in scrambling inside and helping me up, I didn't expect such a petite person. Judging by her cropped, white hair and abundance of laugh lines creasing her face, I'm guessing she might be close to seventy. She's attractive – she must have been quite a beauty when she was young. Her arms are lean and well-toned, the skin wrinkled and tanned. She's wearing a bright yellow, sleeveless shirt with a tie-died swirl of oranges and blues on the front.

"My name's Ruth," she says as she gently examines the back of my head. "That's good – no bleeding. Mind if I look at your upper back?"

After fussing over my scraped shin, Ruth insists on organizing all my food and clothing containers as I instruct her as to where each item belongs. "I love these little A-frames," she says as she sets up the small dining table. "My grandson and his partner have one. They drove out and camped with me for a week this summer. Such sweet boys."

Oh – that kind of partner. How wonderful to have such a loving and accepting grandmother. I'm not sure how many of our generation share her point of view.

"We hiked almost every day, and they taught me how to paddle a canoe," she says, her eyes sparkling. "Just in a calm lake, of course, but I'd like to practice and try a gentle river by next summer. But enough about that. You just relax and I'll be right back."

With a reassuring pat on my hand, she practically bounds out the door. When I enter or exit, I still step carefully, clasping the door frame for balance. My good Samaritan is Wonder Woman.

Moments after she leaves, something catches my eye. A dainty gray cat with a white chest and pale blue collar is perched on my step, peering curiously at me through the open door.

"Well, hello there. Where did you come from, little one?"

I extend my arm downward by my side and wiggle my fingers. "It's okay. Come on in and say hello," I say, keeping my voice soft and gentle.

First one paw tests the next step up, then the other. "Here, kitty," I say.

Ruth's voice catches the cat's attention. "Charli, are you making friends with Ellie?" The animal purrs and bounds over to greet her, then follows her back to the door, leaping inside after her.

"That's your cat, I assume?"

Ruth sets down a shocking pink tote she's brought and a thermos filled with hot coffee. "Yes, this is my travel companion, Charli. She always needs to be in the middle of everything."

She pulls out a bottle of aspirin and a mug, filling it with water from my sink. "I can tell you're hurting," she says as she tips out two pills and hands them to me. Next, she produces another mug, creamer, sugar, banana bread, small paper plates, and napkins from the tote. We share the treats as my head throbs in rhythm. Charli explores my camper for a while, then invites herself to curl up in my lap.

"That's her way of trying to help you feel better," Ruth says.

Slowly petting her silky fur, I say, "I haven't seen anyone traveling with a cat before. Lots of dogs, though."

"She's a great little traveler. She loves perching on my shoulder and wrapping herself around my neck as I walk around. Of course, I have to leave her in the camper a lot of times if I'm going hiking or even visiting places that don't allow pets. She'll perch in a sunny window and watch the world go by."

The vibration of the cat's purring feels soothing.

"I can't thank you enough for rescuing me," I say, but she shakes her head emphatically.

"I'm sure you would have done the same for me. We single ladies have to stick together, help each other out," she says. The expression on my face must reveal my reaction to her wording. Ruth frowns and reaches out a hand to pat mine. "Oh, I'm sorry, dear. I didn't mean to imply that you aren't perfectly capable of taking care of yourself."

"No, it's not that. Not at all. I'm just not used to thinking of myself as *single*." I pause, debating how much I want to tell my extremely new friend. But there's something about Ruth that makes me feel safe. We've just met, but she seems like someone I want to be closer to. I plunge ahead. "Technically, I'm still married. But my husband left me almost a year ago so from that perspective, I guess I could say I'm single."

"Have you filed for divorce?" she asks.

I shake my head. "I keep expecting the other shoe to drop, so to speak. Somebody tracking me down to serve me with papers, or a fat packet showing up in the mail. If that's even how it works." I sigh and take another sip of coffee.

"What about you taking the first step?"

"I guess I'm not ready. Anyway," I say, focusing on folding and unfolding my napkin, "I have no idea where he is. Nobody's heard a thing from him since he left, not even his brother."

"How odd," she says, gazing out the window. "If you don't mind my asking, why do you think he left? Money issues? Other arguments?" She pauses, waiting for my reaction. When I say nothing, shaking my head as I stare at my mug and gently swirl my coffee, she adds, "Another woman? Or man?"

"Well, that's an angle I hadn't even considered. But really, I have no idea. We always seemed to be on the same page when it came to money. We weren't rich, but we were comfortable. At least until the natural disasters, but that's a whole 'nother story. As for arguments, nothing notable. All couples have arguments at times, but I'd say we got along much better than most. I've thought and thought about any disagreements we had in the months before Franklin left, but I can't come up with anything more serious than a silly spat about which movie to watch or him dropping his dirty socks on the floor instead of tossing them in the hamper."

"So ... was he having an affair?"

After ten months of holding all this inside, refusing to share my hurt and confusion with anyone besides Hank –

and only revealing the surface of the churning lake of my emotions – I release the waters from the dam. I pour out my fears, my feelings of betrayal, my loneliness, my anger, my confusion. "I had no idea he was unhappy. Maybe it was an affair. Maybe he wasn't really off playing golf all those times. But," I say, replaying my internal dialogs on the subject, "that doesn't make sense, because it seemed like he was playing *less* often that last month or two. So when would he have met up with another woman? Or man?" I add.

Ruth doesn't shrink away. She listens – truly *listens* – gently prompting me when I stumble, waiting patiently when my throat chokes up too much to speak. We clasp hands across the table and I feel a release – the tension in my entire body that I must have held for all this time begins to relax. Breathing deeply, I feel like it's the first time I've been able to truly fill my lungs in ages.

"Come over to my place for dinner," Ruth says, gathering up her things. "Give me half an hour. Do you drink beer? I'm afraid that's the only liquor I have on hand. Come on, Charli. It's time for your dinner, too."

Although I seldom drink alcohol, but generally prefer wine when I do indulge, a cold beer sounds quite appealing. My headache has subsided a bit and my shin isn't burning like it was before, but booze may tip the scales to dampen both my physical pain and emotional exhaustion. "Beer sounds wonderful. What can I bring?"

She waves me off. "Bring yourself." Then, pausing in the doorway, she turns and smiles, her eyes shining. "I think this is the beginning of a beautiful friendship."

I nod and return her smile. "Here's looking at you, kid," I quip, echoing with another famous line from *Casablanca*.

Chapter 20

Rolling out of bed this morning reminded me of how stiff and sore I got back when I was starting out on this journey, sleeping in the back of the Jeep. My head feels much better, as long as I don't press directly on the spot where the wall hit me, but my scraped shin protested every time I budged during the night and let the sheet move across it. My entire left side aches and when I pull off the baggy t-shirt I slept in, I see purple bruises marking a path from my hip nearly to my armpit. What an idiot to forget to latch the wall in place!

Once I'm dressed, I open all the curtains and relish the warmth of a shaft of sunlight peeking through the branches of the trees. The sky is a glorious shade of blue and other campers are already strolling about in the fresh, clear morning. Looking across the driveway to Ruth's campsite, I chuckle when I spot her outside her trailer, doubled over with her body in a near-perfect A-frame shape, hands and feet set on a neon-green yoga mat, arms and legs straight, butt in the air. Her cat rubs against her arm and gives her an affectionate head-butt.

Trying not to moan out loud as one of my knees protests, I ease myself down my camper's steps and shuffle over to greet her.

"You look like you're trying to imitate my A-Roamer," I say.

With a muffled chuckle, she lowers herself to the matt, face down. "That was Downward Facing Dog, no offense to you, Charli," she says, now using her arms as support as she arches her upper body into another impossibly flexible position. "Cobra," she says. "Hang on, I'm almost done." I watch in awe as she shifts position again, her body now folded up so tightly I think it could roll away if she didn't have her arms extended in front of her. How does she do that? I haven't been that limber since I was twelve.

"And that was Child's Pose," she announces as she unfolds and easily climbs to her feet, running a hand across the top of her cropped hair. "Good morning, Ellie. How did you sleep? How's your head this morning?"

"The head's good, the body not so much. There's nothing like sprawling across a stack of boxes to discover aches in parts I didn't even know I had. I'm definitely feeling my age this morning."

Ruth laughs, a no-holding-back trill of delight. "My dear, have you ever considered becoming a stand-up comedienne? Didn't you tell me you're only sixty-one?"

"That's right," I say, now quite curious about her age. Her skin hints at seventy, but her energy and fitness seem more like early fifties. "So, how old are *you*?" I ask, realizing how much my life story dominated our conversation last night. I hardly know a thing about her.

"What would be your guess?"

I set myself up for that. "I'm terrible at guessing ages." She gestures for me to continue. "Okay," I say, deciding it's better to guess too low than too high. "Sixty-three?"

Her face lights up with delight. "Older. Guess again."

All right, I'll give her my real answer this time. "Seventy."

"Older," she chirps.

"Seventy-five?"

"Older!"

Seriously? This lady who can twist herself into a pretzel and bound up and down stairs is older than seventy-five? I take in her nearly-psychedelic yoga pants and up the ante. "Eighty?" I offer, wondering how that could be possible.

"Not for another two weeks," she replies, beaming.

"No way. You're about to turn eighty? That's amazing!"

"I could be your mother," she says as she steps toward me, arms wide, and wraps me in a gentle hug. "I hope this isn't hurting you," she says, rocking me gently from side to side.

I melt into her touch. Of all the adjustments I've had to make over the past ten months, I think this is what I've missed the most – the warm touch of another human being. Yes, I also miss having sex with my husband – ours was one of those very fortunate relationships where we had a wonderful sex life. But the foundation of that was how often we touched – reaching out to squeeze a hand, Franklin brushing my hair back from my face, lying on his shoulder with his arm wrapped around me, holding me close as we fell asleep at night, our morning hug – so much like this one. I press my face against Ruth's short hair and wrap my arms around her slim body.

We release each other, both grinning. "Wow. I needed that," I say, "but I also need to visit the little girl's room!"

"Oh, that's right. You don't have a toilet in your camper. Well, when you come back, we can talk about our plans for today."

Our plans. I head for the restrooms with a smile so broad my check muscles hurt.

***

I drive as Ruth navigates. Because of my soreness, she proposed we spend time at the Observatory today rather than take one of her favorite hikes in the area. "We'll save that for later in the week," she suggested.

Wanting to learn more about her, I ask Ruth about her family. "You mentioned your grandson. Do you have other grandchildren?"

"Yes, both of my daughters have two kids of their own – all boys. David, my late husband, hoped we'd have a boy and a girl, but he had to wait for boys until our own girls grew up."

"How long were you and David together?"

"We were married forty-nine years. Just missed reaching our golden anniversary. David passed away nine years ago. I stayed in the house for a bit over a year, then decided it was time to sell it and follow our dream of traveling the country. We'd been doing a fair amount of camping when we first retired, planning on hitting the road about six months of the year. But his health went downhill and we had to cut back. After he was gone and I started getting my feet back under me, I decided it was time to get away from that house and all its memories. I haven't regretted that decision."

"Did you already have your cat before your husband passed away?"

"No. I adopted her from the shelter about six months after David died. I introduced her to the camper right away and took her on day trips to the woods only a short distance from our home. She took to it immediately and I knew I had the perfect traveling companion. I didn't care for what her previous owners had named her – Little Bit – so I started calling her Charli, with an 'i'."

Already sensing Ruth's sense of humor, I voice my suspicion. "I'm guessing you've read John Steinbeck's classic. So ... Travels with Charli?"

She chuckles. "Good for you. You'd be surprised how few people pick up on that. Steinbeck had his big poodle and I've got my little kitty. There's more than one way to venture forth in search of America."

***

Late afternoon, Ruth and I join a collection of our neighbors for an informal gathering in the shaded picnic area of the campground. "We're warming up for Saturday night's potluck," a lady named Sally tells me. "You got the flier, didn't you?"

I remember reading that the campground owners host a weekly potluck dinner where they provide burgers and hot dogs and participants bring sides, salads, and desserts. When I checked in, I figured I'd probably skip the get-together. My shyness takes over in large groups of strangers, just the opposite of Franklin, who is a whiz at making friends in any situation – which is why he was such a natural in his sales career. With him by my side, I used to be swept along into conversations with strangers, letting him smooth the way until the ice was not only broken but melted into puddles. Only then did I come out of my shell and join in. Having never talked with anyone in this group before tonight, I would never have joined in if Ruth hadn't coaxed me to accompany her.

Everyone seems to know her already. Ruth introduces me as her "good friend, Ellie" and I feel a swelling of pride. In less than forty-eight hours, I feel closer to her than to anyone I left behind in South Carolina. I relax and start to enjoy the conversations about what everyone did today, favorite places they've visited, and where they call home. We munch on nuts, guacamole and tortilla chips, raw vegetables and hummus (a joint contribution by Ruth and me) and drink beer or wine or lemonade.

When the topic turns to golfing and favorite golf courses, my inner pathetic voice wants me to ask if any of the golf enthusiasts have run across a tall, husky man with thick white hair and a ready smile. Perhaps they might have met him back in the clubhouse, laughing it up with everyone, telling humorous stories peppered with wacky, home-grown sayings. *That's as useless as giving a shark SCUBA lessons* or *You might as well give a sloth a speedboat.* The images in my mind feel almost like recent memories; they're so vivid and detailed it's like I'm watching a movie. I can see him squeezing a man's shoulder, nodding at him in agreement at something he said. There he is, exchanging business cards with someone – and I know they'll actually get in touch again. Now he's waving goodbye as he heads for the door, and a dozen brand new friends return his friendly gesture.

Where is he, right now? Why has he – Mr. Congeniality – never called, texted, emailed, written a letter, sent a postcard – not even to his brother? Why did he walk out on me? Is he still with *her*? Or was there ever a *her*?

Stop doing this to yourself. I offer a polite nod to the circle of strangers and rise to my feet, making eye contact with Ruth, who is sitting across from me. "I'm going back," I mouth, gesturing with a thumb in the general direction of my trailer. When she starts to get up, I force a smile and indicate that she should stay.

"Leaving so soon?" Sally asks.

The line pops into my head and before I can censor myself, I blurt out, "Sorry. Can't stay. Forgot to feed the frog." Like a schoolgirl, I barely suppress a giggle.

Her look of bewilderment threatens to release my laughter, so I hurry toward my campsite, one hand clamped over my mouth, determined not to look back. I walk away swiftly. "I can't believe I just said that!" I say aloud, admonishing myself.

The frog thing was one of our silly little inside jokes – crazy sayings or songs or whatever that most couples seem to collect over the years. We couldn't even remember the origins of many of them, but this was one of our favorite private memories.

Franklin and I were at the movies. Neither of us remembers what we were watching, but we both became far more interested in what his fingers were doing beneath my skirt than what was happening on the screen. It was one of those theaters with stadium seating and not very crowded, so nobody was seated right next to us or close enough behind to see what he was up to. Still, the woman to our left must have heard something, since she *shushed* us rather loudly.

"Let's leave," I whispered in his ear, biting his ear lobe gently and suppressing a moan.

We stood up, Franklin holding the nearly-full box of popcorn strategically in front of his crotch while I carried our large cup of soda pop. The shortest way out was to our left, past the annoyed woman who was seated by herself. Well, it was that or scoot past five people in our row in the opposite direction.

Wouldn't you know it. As my husband stepped in front of the woman, he stumbled, or she tried to trip him – we're not sure. Popcorn spilled on her lap as well as on the heads of the couple in the row in front of us.

"What's wrong with you people?" she hissed.

"Sorry. Forgot to feed the frog," Franklin announced loudly enough for everyone in the immediate vicinity to hear.

We raced out the door to the lobby, laughing like children. "Where do you come up with these lines?" I asked as we hurried to our car.

Like a couple of teenagers, we drove to an undeveloped road and parked behind some bushes, continuing what we'd started, right in the back seat of our newly-acquired Jeep Cherokee – the one sitting in my campsite now.

What happened between us in the nine years since? Up until a few months before he left, everything seemed fine. We still had a great sex life – not as frequent, but we made up for quantity with quality. And then...

Back in the privacy of my own camper, my heartache transforms to bitterness and resentment. *I hope she left you. Left you standing with your jaw hanging open, finally realizing the world doesn't revolve around you and everything you want.*

Again and again, I pace the two steps forward and two back in the cramped space. Tears roll down my face, but they are tears of anger, not sadness. Even in my storm of emotions, I force my voice to a harsh whisper, unwilling to let neighbors hear my tirade.

You really had me fooled, didn't you? Mr. Loving Husband. Mr. Nice Guy. You're nothing but a liar! A fake! I hope you're a million times as lonely as I've been. If you came crawling back to me right now, I'd just turn and walk away and disappear. Then you'd know how it feels.

Screw you, Franklin! No longer caring about what anyone thinks, I shout at the top of my lungs, "Screw you!" I collapse onto a seat and pant, fighting to catch my breath and tame my pounding heart. "Great. Now I've given myself a heart attack," I mutter, snickering at the irony. I snatch a tissue and blow my nose, sounding like a foghorn, then get up and splash water on my face.

Three gentle raps on my door are followed by a familiar voice. "Ellie? It's me. Do you want company?"

Five minutes ago, I would have told her to go away. Now, I realize that Ruth's company is exactly what I need. Opening the door, I feel a wave of calmness begin to pass through my body and mind. Ruth, her cat wrapped around her neck like a shawl, contemplates me with a cautious squint to her eyes. "Come on in," I reassure her. "You and Charli are always welcome."

As tantrums go, this wasn't my worst – not by a long shot. That award goes to the time I've dubbed "Cleaning Day." Franklin had been gone for almost two months and I was sick of being confronted by his clothes hanging in the closet every single time I got dressed. In the first days and even weeks, the clothes he left behind felt like a promise that he would soon come to his senses about whatever the hell prompted him to leave. Surely he would have packed his favorite cardigan sweater – the one with the repaired holes in the elbows. Jeans, shorts, t-shirts, polo shirts. His sport jacket and tailored shirts, slacks and ties, although it's possible he may have taken one from his extensive collection and I wouldn't remember it. Whenever I pictured him stepping through the front door of our apartment carrying his small gym bag and rolling our smallest suitcase, I remember thinking, "He'll be back soon. He's hardly taking anything."

On Cleaning Day, I was ready to purge his belongings that haunted me. Giant black garbage bags in hand, I tore shirts and pants from their hangers, stuffing them into the bags. His beloved and often-mended sweater died a Norman Bates slasher death, victim of my largest and sharpest kitchen knife. It's a wonder I managed not to injure myself. After piling the bags on the curb three days early for trash pickup, I had a change of heart, reverting to poor-little-me,

I-miss-him-so-much mode. I lugged everything back into the house (except for the fragments of the cardigan, of course) and my emotions eventually teetered to a mid-point where I remained rational enough to sift through his belongings, sorting them into "donate" and "toss" piles. The local thrift store was pleased with the windfall.

"Oh. And I sold his golf clubs," I add as I finish telling Ruth the story. I've never before shared that with anyone.

"Oh, my," she says, once again patting my hand in a comforting way. "He'd even left those behind? No wonder you thought he was coming back."

I shake my head slowly, familiar questions ricocheting through my head. "Sometimes I wonder if he meant to return, but something happened to him. Other times I imagine him hooked up with a Sugar Mama, living a fantasy life of resort vacations." My laugh has a bitter tone to it. "Ruth, I'm tired of having my emotions sneak up on me and beat me up. I tell myself to get over it, but how do I manage that? Franklin was a key part of my entire adult life. I don't know who I am as a single woman." Realizing some overlap of her situation with mine, I ask, "How have you managed it? Obviously, I'm not saying that losing your husband is the same as mine walking out on me, but ... you were together for a long time and now he's gone. How do you ...?" I struggle for the words, "... move on?"

As I've talked, the cat has planted herself on my lap. She's been still so far, but now tilts her head up, staring at me, and vocalizes, *mrrr*.

"Charli wants to know if you're okay," Ruth says with a soft smile, "or maybe she's simply asking you to pet her." Letting the tension flow from my neck and shoulders, I stroke the cat's back.

Nodding, Ruth begins. "In some ways, it may have been easier for me to sort through my emotions when David died than it is for you, not knowing if he'll pop up again or why he left in the first place. David was gone and that was that. I had no choice but to begin the process of accepting the fact and moving forward with my life. But, it isn't a straight path to a finish line – not in the least."

Charli bumps my hovering hand with her head, prompting me to continue scratching behind her ear.

"He's been gone nine years, and I still miss him terribly," Ruth continues. "But it's become easier. Early on, I found many memories quite painful. Places we'd visited together, favorite places to eat, a song on the radio – sometimes I felt bombarded by memories that made me want to cry because he wasn't with me to share them again. But now," she smiles warmly, her eyes sparkling, "I'm able to shift my perspective and find joy in remembering as many details as possible and savoring each of those memories."

Her hand flies to cover her lips. "Oh, I'm sorry, dear. That was foolish of me. I imagine your situation is much closer to recovering from a divorce than from a spouse's death. I shouldn't have ..."

"No, Ruth, that's perfectly fine. I know I'm in a somewhat unusual situation, but at times it feels like a death in the family. Other times – like this afternoon – I get angry, wishing we were divorced and that I could forget he ever existed. Argh!" I groan, clasping my hands over my face, "It's so confusing." Charli abandons my lap with an audible complaint.

"And you don't have to figure it out tonight," Ruth says, scooping up the cat. "How about dinner at my place? We can watch a movie afterwards, give your mind a rest."

The old me rears its head. "Thanks, but I —"

"None of that. Come help me fix it. You can chop up veggies for a salad while I cook up some pasta and sauce."

She perches the cat on her shoulder and reaches for my hand. "Come on, now."

If I can't conjure up the "new me" on my own, it's a good thing I've got someone like Ruth along to yank me out of my funk. "All right. I'll bring popcorn," I say, opening one of my food boxes.

Chapter 21

I awaken with a chuckle. My dream fades quickly, other than a clear memory of meandering around the campground holding Charli straight out in front of my body with both arms. I was searching for Franklin, using the cat as a divining rod. After I took a few steps forward, she would swish her tail, utter her little *mrrr* sound, and point a front paw in the direction she wanted me to travel.

If only it were that simple.

It was much cooler last night than it's been – an early hint of autumn approaching. I roll over and flip on the furnace, sighing with pleasure at the luxury of waiting until the tiny room warms up before sliding out from under the blanket. It doesn't take long before my body responds with a heat wave of its own making. I fling back the covers and sit on the edge of the bed, hurriedly turning the furnace off again.

Fortunately, my "personal summers" don't last nearly as long as they did several years ago, but it's hard to tell if my mood swings have also subsided. When I first started going through menopause, I would find myself crying over absolutely nothing. Once, I burst into tears while flipping through a Lands End catalog. When Franklin asked me what was wrong, I sobbed like a young child. "I don't know!

I was looking at all the colors they have for polo shirts and," (sniff, sniff), "look at all these shades of blue!" And I started to wail again. He just held me in his arms, at a complete loss for words.

As I said, I would cry over absolutely nothing. Now, at least, I cry over something tangible.

Soon I'm dressed for a hike with Ruth. She's promised that she's picked out a reasonably short and easy one to start me off. When we meet in front of her camper, she scans me from head to toe. "Ellie, dear, do you have any sort of backpack? Or even a small waist pack?"

Really? "I thought you said this would be a short hike. Do I *need* a backpack?" My concern about my ability to hike with her grows. Ever since she suggested this, I've been imagining her striding far ahead of me and becoming frustrated with how slow I am, although she's reassured me that we'll go at my pace. In other words, we'll emulate the tortoise, not the hare.

"Today's not a problem," she says as she disappears into her trailer. Moments later, she emerges holding a bottle of water and a couple of energy bars, all of which she tucks into her purple pack. "But we need to get you a few basics so we can do longer hikes. If you decide that's what you'd like to do," she adds.

Although I've only taken short walks of under a mile, I've thoroughly enjoyed following a trail into the woods, curious about what views might open up around the next bend, taking in the sounds that we miss when we live in towns, the glimpses of wildlife. I hope I don't let Ruth down if today turns into a disappointing outing with an out-of-shape blob like me.

"Let's get going!" she announces, and we call out our goodbyes to Charli who is curled up in a sunny window of the camper. I think I see the flicker of an ear, but otherwise she ignores our departure.

Arriving at the trailhead, I pause at a sign listing several trail names and distances. "Which one is ours?"

"*Fatman's*," she says, shouldering her pack. "Don't ask me where the name comes from, because I have no idea. Shall we?"

I'm glad Ruth insisted on a fairly early start this morning. The parking lot is filling rapidly and it seems that every fit, young person in Flagstaff plans to hike or run these trails today, despite it being a weekday. I can't imagine what this place was like *before* Labor Day.

The trail starts off fairly flat as it weaves through the Ponderosa forest. Then it begins to climb. I huff my way up each step, stopping to gasp for oxygen about every thirty seconds, moving to the edge of the trail to let others dart past. "You're doing great!" Ruth says as she pauses, waiting for me to catch up. *Damn it, if a woman about to celebrate her eightieth birthday can do this, so can I.*

"Let's take a break here," Ruth suggests, and I sink onto a fallen tree trunk, panting like an old dog. She sits beside me and hands me a bottle of water. "How about this view?" she asks.

I chug the water before looking around. It really is amazing, looking out over the dense forest with peaks rising in the distance. The city blends into the landscape, as if the rocks and trees have barely been disturbed by the presence of humans. Recovered enough to stand, I take several photos with my phone camera. "This is wonderful, Ruth!"

"Are you doing okay? I forgot it was steeper taking the loop this direction. I should have gone the other way around."

"Does that mean we don't have to climb any higher?"

She laughs. "The worst is behind us. It's nearly all downhill from here."

What a relief. "Then I forgive you," I say, grinning.

We set out again, with Ruth pausing to point out a skull-like rock formation. A fit young lady has crawled up inside one of the "eyes" and my fit old friend scrunches into the other. I take their photo. When Ruth and I approach an area where the trail drops down through a series of large rock outcroppings, I'm relieved to discover that the people who built the trail believed in carving steps in the ground rather than expecting a natural-born klutz like me to work my way down a steep slope. We dodge our way amidst smooth boulders carved by the elements in graceful arcs, winding our way through a narrow gap – perhaps the bane of the *Fatman* who gave his name to this trail – and gradually returning to flatter territory.

During the mostly-downhill portion of our journey, I find I'm able to continue hiking without any rest breaks. As the parking lot comes into view, Ruth picks up her pace, no longer concerned that I might melt down into an exhausted heap far from our destination. I think I've just caught a glimpse of her normal cruising speed, and it's beyond my ability. For now.

Tired, but pleased with myself, I join her at the car. "I loved that – thank you!" I tell her.

"I'm so glad," Ruth says, starting the engine. "Now, how about some lunch and then we can shop for a few hiking essentials for you? I know of a couple of stores that have great bargains on new and used outdoor gear."

What did I ever do without her?

Our shopping excursion is a success. I come away with a small backpack, a broad-brimmed hat, and a pair of gently-used hiking boots. A note on the boots explains that they were returned by the original buyer because "they scuff too easily."

"Who worries about a scuff on a hiking boot?" Ruth asks, shaking her head as she rubs her finger over a nearly-invisible mark near the toe of one shoe and examines the sole. "These don't even look like they've been worn outdoors."

I model my selections while walking back and forth in the shoe department, making sure the boots fit comfortably. Although I realize I'll look drab next to Ruth, whose ensemble makes me think of a peacock, I'm pleased to be better equipped for our next hike.

"Are you in any hurry to get back to camp?" she asks as we climb back into her car. Rubbing a hand across her hair, Ruth says, "I'm getting shaggy. I thought I'd try out one of those walk-in hair salons and get a trim."

"That's fine with me. I have nothing else planned."

A quick search on my phone brings up a hairdresser advertising "Walk Ins Welcome" only minutes away. "Clips Ahoy" sounds like it would be a better name for a dog grooming service than a hair salon, but it has a four star rating, so Ruth gives that choice a thumbs up. "All they need is an electric hair clipper with a medium setting. Buzz, buzz and done."

A young woman with eyebrow piercings and about a dozen earrings poking into every curve of her ears nods knowingly as Ruth explains what she wants. "Size three on top," Ruth tells her, "Two on the sides and back. A little longer than yours," she adds, indicating the shaved right side of the girl's hairdo. The top and left side are long.

Another hairdresser is hard at work wrapping strands of a lady's hair in foil, and I suppress a chuckle, thinking about that time I called Franklin from my salon in a panic, realizing my wallet – containing my driver's license, credit cards, and cash – wasn't in my purse. He spotted it on our kitchen counter and drove over to bring it to me. When he walked into the beauty parlor and spotted a client sporting a head covered with layers of aluminum foil rectangles, his eyes opened wide. Whispering to me, he asked, "What the hell are they doing to her? Prepping her for electric shock treatment? Protecting her from an attack from outer space?"

As the stylist shampoos and massages Ruth's scalp, I force myself to stop staring at her tattooed arm. I remove the band holding back my hair, letting it hang loose, and stare at my reflection in the wall of mirrors under the bright salon lights. Ugh. My gray-white roots are a good inch long and my dyed hair hangs shapelessly, its brown color drab and flat. I've let it go, unwilling to fuss with my looks since leaving my apartment, but I hadn't realized quite how unkempt it had become.

Watching the hairdresser rub the top of Ruth's head like she's petting a dog, I make a brash decision. "Can you take me next?"

"You bet. We're almost done here. You want a perm today? Maybe try a new color with highlighting?"

She waves a hair dryer over Ruth's head and brushes the back of her neck with a towel, then whisks off her apron.

"Actually, I'm thinking of going short," I say, feeling slightly breathless with what I'm suggesting. "Not anywhere near as short as hers," I add, quickly, "but ... short-ish. And I want to let my natural color grow out."

She fetches a book from the front waiting area and flips it open to a page of fairly short hairdos. "Maybe a little longer than that," I say. We browse through several more pages until I spot a more mature-looking model showing off an attractive style that looks feminine, yet simple. "Something like this."

The stylist runs her fingers through my hair, studying it. "I think that'll work for you. Come on over to the sink and let's get started."

As she washes my hair, I repeat to myself, "If I don't like it, I can grow it back out. If I don't like it ..."

I keep my eyes closed or avert them to watch Ruth's reaction in the mirror as long strands of hair land on the floor around the chair. Finally, she offers me a hand mirror. "Okay. What do you think?"

The longer I gaze at my hairstyle, mostly-silver with a frame of brown, the better I feel about my new look. I'm even looking forward to a future trim when all the dyed brown can be snipped off. I can't help but think that Franklin would be appalled at seeing me with short hair – he was always suggesting I grow mine even longer, but I found that too much to fuss with. And I'm sure he'd say the silver ages me, despite his own full head of white. *Men.*

Thankfully, he isn't here to offer up his opinion.

"You look wonderful, dear!" Ruth says, hugging me as I rise from the chair.

"So do you." I doubt I could pull off her ultra-sheered look, but on her, it's all energy and *joie de vivre*.

Chapter 22

Life at R-D RV Campground has settled into a comfortable pattern. On alternate days, Ruth and I enjoy some sort of endeavor – usually hiking, but sometimes another kind of touristy activity – and in between, I put in a half day of work, then stroll around the campground, lounge by the pool, relax with a novel. A new proofing job has come in, plus a nibble on yet another, so my sense of panic about my finances has subsided for the time being.

Ruth left early this morning to meet up with an old friend for lunch about ninety minutes south of here. I take advantage of her absence to spend time browsing through shops in Old Town, where I pounce on an adorable pair of earrings shaped like cats. They're simple and colorful; perfect for Ruth's 80th birthday. Before returning to the campground, I stop at a supermarket bakery to order a custom cake, which I'll take to Friday night's camp potluck, the day after her actual birthday. Nothing too large, though. If this week's gathering is like the other two I attended, there'll be a dozen other desserts.

The cute young girl taking my order seems frazzled, strands of blonde hair escaping her hairnet. "So, that's the small sheet, chocolate with whipped frosting. What do you want written on it?"

Almost shouting so she can hear me over the din of PA announcements and a man bellowing into his cell phone a few feet away, I stand on my tiptoes and lean over the display counter. "Happy 80th Birthday, Ruth."

"Hoot?" she responds, frowning as she writes it down.

"Ruth," I repeat. "R-U-T-H."

She spells it back to me and I give her a thumbs up. "I don't need it until Friday afternoon. Can I pick it up around 3?"

"Sure," she says, motioning for me to meet her at the cash register at the end of the counter. After ringing up the sale, she says, "You're all set," and hands me a receipt to bring in when I come back to pick up the cake.

***

"Have you ever gone kayaking or paddle-boarding?" Ruth asks, her voice bubbling over with enthusiasm.

"No, and I've never even considered either one. Nowadays, I'm more of a 'bob-around-in-the-kiddie-pool' sort of gal."

With a wave of her hand, she pooh-poohs my answer. "That's fine for any old day, but I'm talking about doing something *special* for my birthday. There's this beautiful little lake in Prescott I've been reading about. We can rent inflatable kayaks or boards and have a wonderful little adventure."

"Ruth, I'm too ..." I stop, realizing how stupid my excuse was going to sound. *I'm too old.* I almost told an eighty-year-old woman that I'm too old to try kayaking.

She smirks, apparently guessing what I was about to say. "You're too good at paddling to just go out on a calm lake? You're too busy cleaning the house?" she teases.

"I have no idea how to paddle one of those things."

She winks. "Being old has its perks. When I told the young man on the phone that this is for my birthday, I convinced him to come out with us and give us a lesson. No extra charge. I'll bet he's never taught an octogenarian before."

"But what if I fall in?"

"Life jackets," she answers without missing a beat. "Ellie, my dear, let go. Try something new. You're enjoying the hiking, right?"

I nod.

"And think of how much you're improving with that! Remember how winded you were when we hiked Fatman's Loop? And how well you did yesterday? That was twice as long and twice as much elevation gain. You're becoming quite a hiker."

She's right. I'm amazed at how much stronger I've become over the past several weeks of hiking with her. And I'm delighted at how I'm able to fit into smaller size pants. The only downside is that the clothes I have from back when I abandoned my apartment are almost too loose to wear.

"All right, you win. It's your birthday and I'll give it a try," I say. "But I want a boat I can sit down in, not one of those stand-up, balance-y things."

She beams and wraps me in a hug. "Kayaks, then. We'll show that young fellow how badass a sexagenarian and octogenarian can be."

I can't believe she just said *badass*. "Maybe it would be better not to use the word *sexagenarian*. God only knows what he might think that means. It even threw me for a moment."

Laughing, she promises not to put ideas into our young guide's head.

"It's a two-hour drive, so let's plan to leave around 7:30," she says. "We'll paddle and float for a couple of hours, then I've picked out a spot for lunch downtown. We can explore the galleries and antique stores, then drive home before dark."

I'm worn out just hearing about it. No, that's the old me. The new me will have a wonderful time keeping up with my friend who's almost twenty years my senior.

***

Bryce, the guy from the kayak rental shop, is drop-dead gorgeous. Golden brown skin, milk chocolate eyes, and the body of Adonis. Just because I'm almost old enough to be his grandmother doesn't mean I'm dead.

"I'm super psyched to take you ladies out on the lake today," he says as he slides the brightly-colored vessels off the back of his truck. "That's so cool that you're learning to kayak on your eightieth birthday!"

Ruth glows. "My husband and I went on several guided raft trips, but that was a very, very long time ago, back when our girls were teenagers. And I paddled a canoe one time."

The setting is lovely. We're on a ramp that leads to a small alcove of crystal-clear water, pale jumbles of rocks rising on both sides. Bryce has explained that this delightful lake is actually a reservoir, and it's easy to picture what this might have looked like without the water. Stone towers march off into the distance, a maze of walls and slabs, spires and domes, like a natural city of rock built along meandering paths. The water snakes among the formations, offering a mirror reflection of stone and brilliant blue sky.

Squawk! I jump at the raucous shriek of a disturbingly large goose which has plodded up behind me. *Squawk!* It's joined by another, approaching far too closely. I let out an audible whimper and dash around to the other side of the truck.

"Out of here!" Bryce yells at the birds, waving a paddle in their direction. They back off a few feet, then turn toward Ruth.

"You heard him. Back off!" she orders, stomping toward them. Apparently the creatures take her seriously, turning and waddling toward a couple with a small child who are walking along the shore.

I'm so embarrassed that I freaked out like that. I hate geese. I'll never forget that time we were visiting Hank and Cheryl and went to their favorite park for a picnic. After lunch, Franklin and I took the kids over to the lake to feed the ducks while Hank and Cheryl packed up the car. Robbie must have been about three and Lana would have been five. Everything was fine at first – the kids were squealing with delight when the ducks would swim closer, picking out their favorites and trying to toss the bread so only those birds would get a treat. When a few bolder ducks hopped up on shore, Robbie was scared at first, but soon discovered he could run through their midst and they would disperse but return for more.

Then the geese marched over. The ducks scattered and the big bullies dashed toward the kids, like a trio of linebackers rushing the quarterback. The geese screamed and flapped their wings and Franklin snatched Robbie from their attack, swinging him up on his shoulders. "Get in front of Lana!" he shouted, and I grabbed her hand, pulling her behind me so I could act as a barrier between her and the nasty birds. Horrified, I turned away from the screaming geese, wide open mouths revealing rows of teeth. Yes, *teeth*! I scooped Lana up in my arms, and ran, afraid to even look over my shoulder. Finally, Franklin called out, "They turned back," and I sank to the grass, hugging my sobbing niece until her frantic parents arrived to help comfort her. Robbie, however, thought the whole affair was great fun and wanted "Uncle Fank" to give him another horsey ride.

"I hate geese," I mutter.

"Ladies," Bryce says, barely suppressing a smile, "here are your personal flotation devices. Are we ready to play?" He pulls off his t-shirt and I force myself not to stare at his 6-pack abs and bulging shoulders as he changes into a skin-tight, long sleeve top. "To block the sun," he comments as he catches me looking.

He slides a boat to the end of the launching ramp until it's mostly in the water. "Ma'am," he says to Ruth, "climb on in."

Ruth wades a short distance into the shallow water, turns, and plops her rear down into the kayak, rotating her legs in after. With a few wobbles, she's seated against the back rest, and Bryce instructs her on how to position her legs in front of her. He hands her a paddle and pushes her craft fully into the water. Ruth is beaming like a kid in a candy store.

"You're up next," our guide says, positioning another kayak. Imitating my friend, I wade in up to mid-calf and contemplate the considerable drop to the floor of the floating boat. Mentally counting to three, I aim my rear for the center of the kayak and drop. Momentum throws me backward and I find myself mostly on my back, my legs flailing in the air, arms grasping for purchase on the rounded sides of the craft.

Bryce grabs my arm, lifting and sliding my upper body so I'm in some semblance of a seated position. "There you go," he says as I awkwardly wriggle into place. With a death grip, I grasp the paddle he hands me and hold my breath as he pushes me off from the ramp.

"Isn't this great!" Ruth says as she paddles in a slow circle, waiting for us to join her.

I remember to breathe. "What if I fall out? What if my boat tips over?"

"On this calm lake and in those inflatable kayaks, I'd be surprised if you could tip over no matter how hard you try. They're super stable," Bryce says, maneuvering deftly between our boats. "Give it a try."

"What?!"

Ruth is already rocking back and forth, arms set on either side, using her upper body to gain momentum. Her kayak never tilts even forty-five degrees, much less reaching a potential tipping point. Cautiously, I place my arms on the sides of my craft and lean one way and then the other, then put a little more energy into it. I grin in triumph as I realize how hard it would be for me to flip.

Bryce demonstrates how to paddle, suggesting that I grasp mine with my hands farther apart, then leads the way out of the little cove into a wider stretch of water. At first, my full attention is on the angle of the paddle blades as I dip them in the water, right-left-right-left. Ruth and Bryce are moving much faster than I am, but he circles back to me regularly to offer encouragement or a tip on how to make this easier.

"See the falcon?" Ruth calls out, pointing at a bird soaring over the water's surface. We stop paddling and watch it land on a small boulder sticking out of the water like a tiny island. The bird stares across the lake, but I can't tell what it's watching for. Off in the distance, in the opposite direction of the raptor, float dozens of duck-like birds, dark spots in the blue, sparkling body of water.

Bryce leads us into numerous coves and narrow water paths among the pale granite walls rising from the lake. Huddled in cracks and crevices are cactus and low desert bushes, seeming out of place in our watery environment. The scenery is breathtaking.

With tired arms, we eventually paddle to shore and emerge from our kayaks. Diplomatically, Bryce offers each of us a hand to get back on our feet, although I'll bet Ruth could have managed without any assistance. I floundered around like a beached whale just to swing my legs over the side of my boat. There was no way I was going to be able to maneuver my bottom to be higher than my feet without our guide's strong arm to do all the heavy lifting.

"That was wonderful!" Ruth says, wrapping her arms around Bryce's waist for a hug. He laughs and hugs her back.

"Yes – thank you so much," I add, hesitating for a moment, but deciding to go for it. I step forward and hug him as well.

"It was my pleasure," he says, once again changing shirts.

It's certainly our pleasure, too, I think before scolding myself for fawning over a kid in his twenties.

"Ruth," he says – she insisted he stop calling her ma'am – "how do you do it? My grandma is, like, seventy-two or something, and there's no way she'd try kayaking or go out hiking like you do."

I'm sure she's asked this all the time, but she pauses a moment before answering. "Well, a lot of it is good luck, I suppose. I've stayed pretty healthy over the years and haven't had any serious injuries. But I think a big reason why I've stayed healthy is because I didn't listen to people who told me I was getting to be too old to do this or that. I don't believe in stopping the activities I enjoy just because someone says I *should*. Now, if I *try* something and find that I simply *can't* do it anymore, that's another matter."

Sad to say, I've been guilty of this. Flo from my book club once announced that she wanted to sign up for climbing lessons at the local recreation center. "Like, climbing straight up the wall with ropes?" I asked, astonished that a woman of sixty-three would even consider such a thing. "Are you nuts? You'll break your neck. We're too old to be trying daredevil sports like that."

The good news is that Flo went anyway, didn't break her neck or any other body parts, and apparently enjoyed it thoroughly. At the time, I thought she had lost her marbles. Now, I'm reconsidering.

"She's like a fountain of youth," I tell the young man. "Look what she's got me doing! A year ago, I would never have imagined I'd find myself hiking up mountains or floating around in a large rubber ducky."

Ruth adds one more thing. "If I had to sum up my 'health secret' with just one word, it would be *enthusiasm*. That's what keeps me going. I find things I love to do and seek out new experiences, and I'm excited about what each day might bring."

"You should start a video channel and teach people what you know," Bryce says, tying a final knot in the straps he's used to secure the kayaks on the back of his truck again. "I'd get my grandma to watch and I'll bet she'd tell all her friends to subscribe."

Ruth chortles. "I'll give that some thought, Bryce. I could be the next Jack LaLanne. *The Ruth Erlich Fountain of Youth Show*," she says, sweeping a hand as if reading the words from a marquee. "That has a nice ring to it."

"Rock on." He's on board, even though I'm sure he has no clue who Jack LaLanne was.

Chuckling, I ask, "Do we have time to stop for lunch before the ceremony for your star on the Hollywood Walk of Fame?"

"Oh, I think we might be able to fit that in." We wave goodbye to Bryce and walk arm-in-arm to our car. "You know," she whispers, "he needs to give a warning if he's going to whip off his shirt like that. He almost gave me a heart attack – and that would have been the end of my fountain of youth career."

We giggle like schoolgirls the rest of the way to lunch.

Chapter 23

Happy birthday, dear Ruth, happy birthday to you!

I barely got back in time after getting the Jeep's oil changed, which took far longer than I expected, and picking up the birthday cake. And I totally forgot about candles. Before I could even unload her cake from its box, our camp hosts, Rosie and Danny, announced Ruth's birthday to the weekly potluck crowd and led all of us in song.

I raise my hand as if I'm in school and stand up. "Everybody, be sure to save room for a slice of birthday cake," I announce as I ease the cover from the box. Even from my vantage point, I can see that the dessert table is loaded with other options, but I've seen a few of these folks chow down at previous potlucks, so I'm sure they'll make a significant dent in my offering.

With the cake finally revealed, I realize something is amiss by the puzzled expression on Ruth's face. The others at our table lean in and stare at it and I take a good look for the first time.

> Happy 80th Birthday
> Are you the 8th?

"The eighth *what*?" a woman asks.

What the hell? "That's not what I ordered. I even spelled out your name for them," I say to Ruth, who is smiling but shaking her head in bewilderment.

Rosie has joined us at our table. "I don't get it. '*Are you the 8th?*' What does that mean?"

Are you the 8th? Are you the 8th?

People are muttering the question when the birthday girl suddenly claps her hands and flings her arms in the air as if signaling a touchdown. "I got it!"

"And?" I prompt.

"R. U. T. H. What do the kids text when they're abbreviating the words 'are you'?"

"R U," we answer in chorus, one lady drawing the letters in the air.

She nods. "Right – so T-H sounds a bit like 'the 8th'. R-U-T-H becomes Are You The Eighth."

I knew that clerk in the bakery wasn't the sharpest knife in the drawer. I cover my face with both palms, shaking my head "I think you might be right."

"Hey, folks," Danny shouts as people line up at the food tables, "special treat tonight. George is providing bratwurst, so decide if you want a brat or a burger when you swing around to the grill."

A short, jolly-looking, white-bearded man who would be a natural to play Santa waves at the crowd, both hands clasping plastic-wrapped packages of sausages. Danny hands him a kitchen knife, and George goes to work freeing the brats from their shrink-wrapping, piling them on a plate to carry over to the grills.

Standing in line to fill my plate, I hear a commotion. I turn to see Danny and George running around, waving their arms in the air and someone points at a raven perched on a tree branch above the picnic area.

"He stole a brat!" George yells, pointing an accusing finger at the bird. Indeed, it has a bratwurst clamped in its beak.

The large black bird leaps into the air, flapping its long wings slowly. Flying directly overhead, we hear a raspy *croak*, and a large piece of the sausage splats into the green Jello mold, takes a bounce like it hit a trampoline, and lands on a woman's plate. "That's disgusting!" she shrieks, dropping the loaded plate on the ground, spreading baked beans, cole slaw, salad greens, and potato chips everywhere. A black Labrador pulls his leash free from where it was tied to a table, and devours the mess like a wet-vac. Charli, who has been strolling around the area exploring rocks and pine cones, scrambles ten feet up a Ponderosa pine and glares back over her shoulder at the dog, which is paying her no attention. Emboldened by the distraction, a second raven swoops down and nabs an entire, unopened package of bratwurst. George, Danny, and another man scurry back to the grills, positioning themselves to guard the remaining meat from further raids.

After the rest of the Jello is disposed of and the remaining bratwurst is safely cooking on the grill under guard and the dog has been removed to his own campsite, things settle down. Ruth is regaling everyone at our table with the story of our kayaking excursion yesterday when I hear a shrill series of calls and spot both ravens circling overhead. One lands on the camp road, not twenty feet from where Charli is sitting.

The cat's tail swishes swiftly side-to-side as the two similarly-sized creatures stare each other down. Charli goes into a low crouch and inches toward the bird, which turns and waddles away from her, vocalizing loudly, before reversing course and heading straight toward her. Charli stands her ground until the raven takes to the air, landing behind her. She spins to face it again. The second bird flutters from one tree to another, intently focused on the action below.

"Should I go rescue her?" I ask Ruth, worried that the two large birds might attack Charli.

She shakes her head. "She'll figure things out," she says, taking another bite of her cake. "Mmm. This is quite good."

Charli creeps toward the bird again, but this time its mate swoops down from the tree, passing only a few feet above the cat's head. She's off like a bullet, taking shelter under our table, surrounded by a protective fence of human legs. I peer down at her and she appears totally relaxed, calmly washing her chest like nothing is amiss, her head bobbing up and down as her pink tongue combs and cleans her fur.

"See?" Ruth says. "She learns quickly."

***

After another enjoyable hiking day, Ruth and I wind down the evening at her place, half-watching Animal Planet while we chat. Charli is crouched on a cushion in front of the television, her mouth trembling in excitement as a school of fish dash about on the screen.

"Time flies so quickly," Ruth says. "I can't believe I've been in Flagstaff almost three months already. It's almost time to pack up and move south."

"You're leaving Wednesday, right?" God, I'm going to miss her.

She hears the sadness in my voice. Reaching for my hand, she says, "I can't begin to tell you how much I've enjoyed spending time together. I've grown comfortable with my solitary lifestyle, but knowing I have a good friend nearby makes a world of difference."

I blink back tears, determined to emulate her, to grow comfortable with my own company as well. "Same here," I manage.

Ruth takes my face gently in both hands. "Ellie, dear, I don't want you to change your travel plans, but I would be delighted if you could come down to Tucson at some point this winter while I'm there."

I don't know whether to laugh or cry with joy. "I've been going in circles about my travel plans so much that I've given myself vertigo. I'd love to come join you. I just don't want to become a pest or seem like a stalker or something."

"Oh, Ellie," she says, pulling me forward for a kiss on my forehead. "Don't you know I love you? I'm thrilled that we'll be able to continue our adventures together."

We wrap our arms around each other and I tell her that I love her, too. Charli nuzzles her way in between us, eager to join our mutual admiration society.

Dabbing my eyes, I ask, "Remember how I thought bad luck comes in threes?" Ruth nods. "Well, I think I'm in a good luck streak now. The first lucky thing was my camper," I say, ticking it off with one finger. "I was so fortunate to find a great deal that I could afford, and I love living in it. Did I tell you I'm changing its name?"

"To...?"

"My *Great Escape*," I say, grinning. "It was the key to escaping my bad luck. Anyway," I raise a second finger, "the second *very* lucky thing was meeting you."

"I feel the same. And what's the third bit of good luck?" she asks.

I shrug my shoulders. "The third is yet to come."

I suggest we celebrate my future good luck and our reunion in Tucson with ice cream. I fetch a carton of Cherry Garcia from my freezer and return to Ruth's camper, where the three of us – two with spoons and one with her rough little tongue – manage to devour the entire pint.

"I think my blood sugar just went through the roof," I say, flopping back on the sofa with a satisfied sigh, but the look of dismay on Ruth's face reveals that she's taken me seriously. "I'm sorry, Ruth. Did I say something …?"

"Oh, it's nothing, dear," she says, but her face is clouded, drawn. She turns away.

"What is it?" I ask.

With a deep sigh, she straightens her back and faces me again. "Don't mind me. Sometimes a memory just pops up and slaps me right across the face, even after all this time."

I certainly know how that feels.

She continues, "Did I ever tell you about how my David died?" I shake my head. "Officially, he died from hitting his head after a fall in the shower."

I gasp. "How awful!"

"But that doesn't tell the whole story," she says. "Now, I know it's not unusual for older people to fall in the shower. But David had developed Type 2 Diabetes, you see. After he retired at 65, he decided he was too old to take long hikes any longer. After another year or so, I couldn't even convince him to go for short hikes or walks around the neighborhood. He gained weight, sat in front of the television all evening. When he was diagnosed, the doctor gave him guidelines on diet and exercise, and he would follow them for a week, then go right back to his unhealthy habits." She shakes her head. "I didn't want to be a nag, but it was so hard seeing him change like that.

"Over time, the nerves in his feet were affected. His balance became quite poor, so we installed grab bars in the shower, but…"

I hold her hand. How difficult that must have been for Ruth, with all her energy and vigor, to witness her husband becoming less and less interested in doing the things they had enjoyed together, and to watch his health fail.

With an energetic slap of her palms on her knees, she rises to her feet. "We can't change the past," she declares, "only learn from it. But we can shape the future. So – are you up for a visit to the Grand Canyon tomorrow? I know that's two hiking days in a row, so we could wait…"

I've just completed a proofing job and I'm waiting on a client for an updated draft. "No – I'm in. Let's do it."

"We'll want to leave early. I don't think we'll have enough time to hike down to Indian Garden and back out, but we'll go as far into the canyon as makes sense. I can't believe you've never been there before. Trust me, photos don't do it justice."

I can hardly wait!

Chapter 24

It felt like a piece of my heart was torn from my chest as I watched Ruth drive off, her trailer's slide-outs tucked away, the campsite where I spent almost as much time at as mine now sitting naked and empty.

Unsure how I want to spend my day, I stroll the loop around the camp, walking more slowly than usual. There are a few people who seem to spend all their time here, seldom leaving the campground for more than a quick trip to the store for groceries, but most of the sites are silent, their occupants off on some jaunt. I've grown to rely on spending time with Ruth, but now that I'm here without her for the next ten days, I really should make an effort to get to know some of my neighbors, and not only at the weekly potlucks.

There may come a day when Ruth won't be in my life. There's the obvious, of course – she's almost twenty years older. Not only is it likely I'll outlive her, but she may not always remain healthy enough for this lifestyle. Or we might grow tired of being around each other.

Look at how things went with me and Franklin. Till death do us part, and all that. After we left California, I let my attachments to those friends fade away and I never tried all that hard to connect to anyone new in South Carolina. I had my husband as my best friend, and I thought that was enough. Until it wasn't.

The new me needs to learn to reach out to people more. Especially if I'm going to be moving from place to place.

Continuing on my stroll, I wave and say hello to Howard. As he has every day since I've been here, he's sitting sentry under a large, patched-up shade that extends from his ancient camper. Since I pass by his place every time I walk to or from the restrooms, we greet each other multiple times per day.

Today, I decide to deviate from my usual pattern by stopping and actually attempting a conversation with the man.

"How are you today, Howard?"

His eyes open wide in astonishment. "Well, young lady, I'm doing just fine. How about you?" He smooths his abundant mustache and rubs a hand across his mostly bald scalp.

"Doing well, thanks. I was just admiring your camper. Are you the original owner?"

"Sure am. Bought her in 1969, right after I got back from 'Nam. We've been everywhere together, Delilah and me."

"Oh, I guess I haven't met your wife. Is she here?" I ask, squinting through the open door of his trailer.

"My wife?" He chortles, a deep belly laugh. "I can't picture any woman on this green earth who'd marry a misfit like me."

"Your ... friend, then?" His amusement grows – he shakes his head and wipes his eyes in glee.

"Delilah's my trailer," he says, then bursts into song, "*My, my, MY Delilah! Why, why, WHY, Delilah?*" He gestures broadly with his arms as he really gets into the number, bellowing out the high notes.

It sounds familiar, like something I may have heard on the radio when I was a kid. Howard shows no signs of ending his rendition of the golden oldie, moving on to a second and then a third verse. Realizing the song is about a jilted lover showing up at Delilah's door with a knife in his hand, *"...and she laughed no more...,"* I manage a broad smile as I back away.

"Got to go," I say, waving. "Nature calls." I turn and walk briskly to the ladies room where I stand at the sink, splashing cold water on my face. After several minutes, I slip back outside and circle around to the campground office.

I'm relieved to see Rosie behind the counter. "'Morning, Ellie. What can I do for you?" Before I can decide just how I should word my question about Howard, she adds, "Are you feeling all right? You look a bit pale."

"No, well, I was just, uh, chatting with Howard and I — well, he was telling me about his camper. Did you know he calls it *Delilah*?"

With a raise of her chin, Rosie mouths *ah*. "Did he happen to do his Tom Jones impression?"

Now I remember – that was the singer's name. "Yes, he did. The entire song."

"And you're wondering if you need to worry about him, especially around knives." She chuckles. "Danny once suggested we post a sign by his site, like 'Howard doesn't bite'. I know Howard's a bit different, but he's just a big, ol' Teddy bear. He's been staying with us during the warm months for at least the past dozen years. He's as harmless as a kitten – that sweet little Charli was probably more dangerous than ol' Howard."

I let out a long *whew*. "Good to know. Now I'm embarrassed that I took him for a mad slasher. Maybe I'll go back and chat with him some more."

She smiles. "I'll bet he'll really appreciate that. Just so you know, he loves to sing, so be ready for something to remind him of another favorite song."

"I'll do that. Actually, he's got a pretty good voice."

Stopping off by Howard's site again on my way back along the loop, we end up having a fascinating conversation about local birds and how climate changes are affecting migratory patterns. Not only does he perform a lovely rendition of "Blackbird" by the Beatles, he also seems to be able to imitate the calls and songs of a few dozen birds.

Eventually, I excuse myself. I think he would have gladly talked with me the entire day, but I do need to spend a few hours working. Before doing that, I complete my walking loop, stopping briefly to share greetings with a foursome – including campground owner Danny – playing cards. I've seen them gathered around a table every morning I've been around camp.

"Where's your cat today?" one of the women asks.

Danny pipes in, "No, no, Margaret. That wasn't Ellie's cat. It belonged to Ruth. She checked out this morning."

"Oh – the lady who just turned eighty? I thought she was your mother."

"A close friend," I answer. "We'll be meeting up again in Tucson." I feel myself beaming.

Margaret nods. "I guess you two don't really look much alike, but I thought, with your age difference, she'd have to be family. Why else would you want to spend time with an old—"

"Age is just a number – it's not important," I say, thinking about Ruth's story the other night.

She raises one eyebrow as if she finds my answer questionable.

"I'd better let you get back to your game," I say, moving away. There's no rule saying I have to make friends with *everyone*.

As I open the door to my camper, a sizeable motorhome rumbles its way into Ruth's former pull-through campsite. I watch as two strangers emerge from the shiny contraption, buzzing around its perimeter as they prepare to settle in. Compartments glide out on both sides, hoses are laid out across the ground like umbilical cords, and the entire bus-like vehicle hums and hisses as leveling jacks emerge underneath and shift the unit until it is in perfect balance. Realizing that I'm staring, I retreat into my camper. I'll go say hello once they're not so busy setting up. Maybe that will give me time to stop feeling like they are intruders who've invaded Ruth's home.

Not long after I sit down at my computer to work, I hear a car start up and the grumble of tires on gravel. Looking out a window, I see that my new neighbors have already driven away in the compact car they were towing behind their motorhome.

***

Why am I nervous? I've got Nan Uchida's number called up in my phone, but I hesitate to press the "call" button. *What will I say to her?* This is silly. How many times did Nan, Claire and I stroll along curving roads near our California homes, talking about neighborhood gossip, their kids, our work, our husbands, even our sex lives? I can picture us along with our husbands sitting in our den eating popcorn, praising or criticizing this month's shared movie, which always segued into discussions about politics (fortunately, we all had similar leanings), religion (with respectful, yet divergent beliefs), and sports (where the arguments were most heated).

Last I heard, she and Peter moved to San Francisco after the fire. Disappointment hits me when I hear the recorded message that the number I called is no longer in service. Remembering that the last email I tried sending her bounced, I brush off that old feeling of despair I felt when my attempts to contact Franklin by phone and email failed.

Move on. I look up Claire Williamson's number. Sadly, Claire and I have only spoken once by phone since the fire, and our emails back and forth faded away as she and Otis got busy rebuilding and Franklin and I became more involved with our new acquaintances in South Carolina.

I press the green button and listen to it ringing.

"Ellie," she answers, "is it really you!?"

Good old caller ID. "It's really me. Hey, you sound just the same. How are you?"

"Great! It's good to hear from you. Are you guys still on the east coast?"

And with that, we have our opening topic. Claire is shocked to hear about Franklin's Disappearing Act. "I would never have pictured him as the type to pull a stunt like that." She sounds even more amazed that I'm on a solo Great Escape. "Seriously, Ellie? You always seemed like the most *settled* one of our bunch."

"Settled?" I ask.

"That's probably not the best term for it. More comfortable being at home than going to new places? Someone who likes things to be predictable?"

"Kind of a *home-body*?" I ask, cringing at the images this brings to mind, but realizing she's not far off the mark. I *was* pretty set in my ways, preferring the tried-and-true to the unknown.

"I suppose," she says, "but in a *good* way. Being uprooted by the fire was difficult for everyone, but I think it may have been harder for you than it was for me."

I hadn't thought of it that way before. Could my reactions to our forced relocation be a clue to Franklin's dramatic exit fifteen months later?

Stop that, Ellie. No more hashing out why he left. Move on.

I steer the conversation to the present, asking about their new house and reminiscing about the people who used to live near us in the valley. What became of the Newtons? ("No idea.") Have you been in touch with Nan and Peter? Her phone number and email both must have changed. ("We've fallen out of touch.")

At least I'm not the only one.

"What's next for you?" she asks. "Doesn't Flagstaff get cold in the winter?"

"I'm moving south to Tucson in a week or so to meet up with a wonderful new friend who's been getting me out hiking and even kayaking."

"Good for you! Ellie, it sounds like you've really made the best of a bad situation. I know you used to talk about going on camping trips, but Franklin was just lukewarm about the idea. You know, Otis and I have a vacation planned to Phoenix in November. Maybe we can get together, go out to dinner, see a movie?"

"I'd love that. It would be great to see you again."

When we end the call, I feel good about having reached out to an old friend. She sounded like she genuinely wants to get together. I should have called her ages ago.

Chapter 25

I've just settled down in my newly-acquired camp chair to read a book when Rosie walks up.

"Oh good, you're home. I was just stopping by to leave you a note that you got a package today in the mail. Come by the office and we'll have it for you." She peels a sticky note off a pad in her hand and stuffs it in her pocket.

"Thanks," I say as she heads off toward another site.

A package? My stomach clenches. I'm not expecting anything from Hank – we just talked a few days ago and he had nothing of importance to forward to me. If Franklin contacted him to find out where I am, but asked him to keep his call a secret, would Hank have told me?

My hands sweating, I walk as swiftly as I can to the office. "Howdy, Ellie," Danny says as the bell rings when I walk through the door. "Rosie sent you for your mail, I see." He produces a box from behind the counter and sets it in front of me. It's slightly larger than a ream of computer paper. I peer at the return address.

Hamner and Lowenstein, 54 Broad Ave., Beltain, Ohio.

Oh, God. It sounds like a legal firm. Franklin is filing for divorce.

But when I pick up the box, it's light as a feather. Puzzled, but still dreading what might be in the package, I thank Danny and hustle back to the privacy of my camper. As carefully as my trembling hands will allow, I slice through the tape sealing the box shut and lift the lid.

Bubble wrap – the kind with the tiny bubbles. Nobody would cushion paperwork in bubble wrap, would they? Like peeling an onion, I pull back layer after layer, starting to wonder if there's anything else in the box other than the protective plastic. Finally, I discover a small, white box nestled like a precious egg.

The memories rush back of another large box displaying the logo of my favorite department store. Franklin and I had been dating for almost two years, pretty much living together for the previous six months. He still had his apartment, but spent most nights at mine. One Saturday night, after we went out for dinner at our favorite Italian restaurant, he insisted that we swing by his place so he could pick up something he needed.

He invited me up, which seemed odd since he always spent the night at my place over the weekends. When I walked in, he disappeared into his bedroom for a minute, emerging with a white box. "Just a little something I picked up for you," he said, leading me to the couch before setting it on the coffee table in front of me. "I hope it's the right size."

"What's the occasion?" I asked.

"Does there have to be a special occasion for me to give my girl a present?" He sat beside me and kissed my cheek.

"I guess not," I said, feeling delighted. What could it be? Like a kid at Christmas, I picked it up and shook it gently, listening for any clue. It was very lightweight. I had thought it might be a sweater or blouse, but it didn't seem heavy enough. Unless it's silk – I've always wanted a genuine silk shirt. Or maybe it's a scarf?

"Are you planning on opening it anytime soon?" he asked, laughing.

"Yes, of course." I eased the lid open and began turning back the folds of tissue paper. And more folds. And more.

Knowing Franklin's offbeat sense of humor, I began to suspect that there was nothing in the box at all. But then I uncovered a tiny, black jewelry box. "Oh!" Could it be ... ?

Taking the box in hand, Franklin opened it as he dropped to one knee. "Eleanor Jean Driskel, will you make me the happiest man on earth? Will you marry me?"

With a lump in my throat at the memory, I pause in unwrapping my mystery package and gaze out the window of my camper, focusing on a woman walking her dog around the loop. Convinced that this box came from Franklin yet uncertain what his intent might be, I open the little white box.

Inside is a nylon draw bag. And inside that – I pull out a long, ribbon-like strip of fabric and a black plastic device labeled "LED – Hi / Lo / Off."

"Ruth," I say aloud. "This is from Ruth."

I had admired her lighting strip that she used to gently illuminate her steps and banister leading into her camper. We looked for something similar in the stores around Flagstaff one afternoon, but I didn't like the lights we found. She must have ordered one like hers and had it shipped to me here.

Laughing at how I'd worked myself into such a tizzy, I call her to thank her for the gift and to share my crazy story with her.

***

Without Ruth here to take the lead on what to do when I'm not working, it would be very easy to revert to my couch potato days, spending my day puttering around camp, visiting with neighbors, reading, and running an errand or two in town. But after the past two days of that, I miss getting out in the fresh air, enjoying the sights and sounds of nature, and – I realize with shock – the sensation of working my legs and breathing harder as I challenge my body to walk farther and climb higher than I could have imagined a few months back.

Without a hiking companion, it takes a conscious effort for me to stuff snacks and water into my pack, climb into the car, and drive to a trailhead. This morning, determined to begin, I forced myself to get out of my camper at a reasonable hour and I returned to where my hiking excursions in the area first began. Fatman's Loop, here I come!

Remembering all too well how exhausted I felt after climbing the steep parts of the trail, I set out at a modest clip, saving my energy for the hard part. When I reach an uphill section, I slow my pace just enough so I can maintain my speed and still be able to speak – a trick that Ruth taught me for hiking up a long rise. Finding my rhythm, I enjoy looking around as I climb, discovering interesting rock formations and views of the valley below that I never noticed our first time out.

In what seems like no time at all, I realize I'm at the high point of the loop. I'm breathing hard, but definitely not gasping for air like I was weeks ago. Grinning like a crazy woman, I continue my hike, delighted to be comfortable enough to admire the forest flora, discover a red-breasted woodpecker hammering a tree overhead, and even to scan the surrounding forest a bit nervously when I come upon a collection of scat that clearly resembles the droppings of a house cat, only considerably larger. Mountain lion? Bobcat? Remembering a sign that suggested that the big kitties will usually avoid humans, I burst into song. "*My, my, MY Delilah!*" I can't help it – I've had that ear worm ever since I met Howard and his trailer.

A man near my age appears around a bend in the trail, climbing up toward me and I go silent. He raises one eyebrow as we pass and I offer him a polite nod, wondering if my face is as flushed as I think it is. As I descend around the switchback and continue on the trail just below him, I hear him singing, "*Why, why, WHY, Delilah?*" Laughing aloud, I continue humming the song, almost skipping in time to the tune.

Thinking back on the months since my husband left, I can't believe how much more energy I have now. An observer could have tracked my mood swings from being sad and heartbroken versus angry and resentful by the fluctuations in my eating patterns. When I was depressed I ate, putting on pounds so easily I could have been a model for the Michelin Man. During my spells of temper tantrums, I had to force myself to remember to eat.

Judging by the way my clothes fit, I probably weigh less now than I have in several years. I'm nowhere near my high school size, but who is? Okay, so maybe Ruth might be, but still I'm feeling pretty good about myself. It's been a long time since I could say that.

Before heading back to camp, I stop in at the Flagstaff Visitor Center where I pick up literature and maps for additional hikes in the area. There's a fit-looking couple I met yesterday – Carlton and Kari – who had just arrived at R-D RV Campground and told me they planned to visit some of the National Monuments in the area. Maybe I'll invite them to hike with me in the next day or so in Walnut Canyon. The cliff dwellings sound like they'll be quite different from the ones I saw early in my trip, and the name

"Island Trail" intrigues me. A steep descent into the canyon of nearly 200 feet, including many stairs? I can do that.

Chapter 26

After a month in one place, I'm starting to feel like a pro at living the camping life. I've found a place for everything and with such a compact living area, I keep everything in its place. I've learned the quirks of keeping the refrigerator at the right temperature, how long it takes to heat up water on the stove, how to create a comfy spot to curl up to read. But I barely remember how to break it all down to move on to a new location.

Determined not to mess up like I have in the past, I study the checklist from the Feddersons. It seems like I bought my A-frame from them ages ago, but it's only been about six weeks. Before I begin the process, I grin while crossing off their heading of *Preparing Little Roamer for the Road* and changing it to read *Preparing for my next Great Escape*.

Backing my SUV into place and latching the trailer to it goes reasonably well. I've already checked off all the steps for stowing everything inside the camper that might shift around during travel, so I think it's time to collapse the walls.

"Hey, Ellie – are you heading out?"

"We came to say goodbye."

Carlton and Keri from the Walnut Canyon trip last week come over and hug me. "It was fun hiking with you guys," I say. "Let's keep in touch."

"Absolutely," Carlton says. "You've got our card. Like we said, let us know if you're coming to the Bozeman area. Yellowstone is amazing in the winter, if you've never been. Give us a bit of notice and we can arrange to get off work and go snowshoeing to some wonderful spots."

Seeing the expression on my face, Keri adds, "Or we can show you around during the summer."

"That sounds like a more likely plan," I say. "Or maybe we can meet up somewhere during our travels. I haven't made any decisions beyond going to Tucson for the next month, so let me know where you're off to. I'm flexible."

Another voice calls out, "You leaving?"

I can't remember the man's name, but he was at my table at last week's potluck. "Yep. Driving to Tucson today."

"I've always wanted to see how these little A-frames fold down," he says. "Mind if I watch?"

"Not at all." I won't let an audience deter me from referring to my checklist every step of the way.

Tweeee! With an ear-splitting whistle, the guy – Melvin? Marvin? Erwin? – summons anyone within ear shot to "Come check this out!" Several neighbors wander over to see what's going on. "She's going to fold it up!" he announces as if he were introducing a magic act.

I decide to play along. "Is everybody ready?" I ask as I stand in the doorway of my camper. Another woman calls out "Wait! Wait for me!" as she and her dog shuffle toward my campsite. I give her a moment, then declare, "Here we go."

As I lower the first of the triangle walls, my audience – now grown to at least eight people – offers appreciative *oohs* and *aahs*. Melvin/Marvin/Erwin asks to see how I unlatched it before folding it down, and that leads to multiple people wanting a demo. I raise the wall back into place so they can take turns stepping inside to watch how the latches work. "What you don't want to do when you're setting it up," I explain, "is forget to latch one side before turning to do the other." Although it's a hell of a way to meet friends.

Once I step outside and fold down the final two ceiling pieces, I earn a standing ovation. My self-appointed emcee asks if I'll set it up again so he can see the entire process, but Carlton comes to my rescue. "I'm sure Ellie needs to be getting on her way. Thanks for the demo." He and Kari manage to politely herd everyone away so I can focus on finishing my preparations.

With a final walk around my vehicle and trailer to double-check that everything is good to go, I climb aboard and pull out of the campground, back to checking my mirrors every five seconds to make sure my Great Escape is escaping with me.

***

The transition from the Ponderosa forests of Flagstaff at nearly 7,000 feet elevation south through the mountains, then descending steadily for 6,000 feet to the Phoenix desert has been dramatic. As the elevation drops, the temperature climbs. Evergreen trees disappear, replaced by iconic saguaro cacti, giant sentinels of the desert pointing multiple curved arms toward the sky.

Thank God today is Sunday. Ruth warned me that the traffic through Phoenix would be heavy and suggested a longer route that circles around much of the metropolitan area, avoiding the most congested sections. If this is what's considered light traffic, I can't imagine what it's like driving through the middle of the city during the work week.

I drive as far to the right as possible, keeping an eagle eye out for places where the lane I'm in is required to exit. Cars weave around me, jumping in and out of lanes like balls careening wildly around a pool table after a powerful break shot. It's impossible for me to see what's happening with traffic directly behind me, which is probably a good thing for the sake of my sanity, although my frequent glances at my side mirrors are nerve-wracking enough.

After what seems like hours, the traffic thins and I realize I've reached the southern outskirts of the Phoenix area. The speed limit jumps, but I settle in at 65 and keep to the right. The desert is remarkably flat, but along the way craggy peaks pop up here and there like islands. As I enter the Tucson area, palm trees rise above the neighborhoods. Relieved to finally exit the interstate, I wind my way along tree-lined boulevards and past homes whose landscaping relies heavily on white and red decorative gravel, broken up by flowering bushes and cacti. When my GPS announces, "Your destination is on the right," I almost cry with relief. I can't wait to get settled into a new home base.

After registering, I'm led to my pull-through site by Roger, whose only words to me before he hopped into his golf cart were, "You're on Roadrunner Way." We weave down one lane and up another until he swings into site number 52, a wide passageway between lanes with hedges growing along each side. As I start to pull in, he waves and takes off without a glance back.

Okay. Get out the checklist. Do *not* unhook without blocking the trailer wheels. Do *not* drop a wall on your head.

I pull up on one of my blocks to level the trailer side-to-side. Check. I put the chocks against the wheels. Check. I unlock the hitch and crank the jack to unhook the trailer from my car. Check. Unhook the chains and everything else connecting the two vehicles. Check. I pull the Jeep forward a few feet so I can level the trailer front-to-back. Check. Adjust the jack until level. Check.

Uh oh. I'm just about to start raising the roof and walls when I notice how far the trailer is from the water and electrical hookups for my site. Glancing around at neighboring campers, I realize that most are parked close to the left side of their sites, where the utilities are. I'm closer to the right, crowding out my picnic table. I retrieve my white hose from its storage area and, sure enough, it won't reach the spigot.

Do I move my camper or buy a longer hose?

With a sigh, I decide to do it right. After all, I'm planning on being here for at least a month. Pulling out my other checklist – the one for breaking down my camp – I begin again. Back up the car, hook up the trailer, remove the wheel chocks, drive around the campground loops until I can circle back into my site again, pull in to the left half of site 52, get out and check that I'm in a good position, pull forward another eight feet, check again. Got it.

I add more notes to my checklists.

Once everything is set up again and I've crossed all the t's and dotted all the i's, I collapse on my bed.

"Ellie? Are you here?"

Ruth's voice is like a magic elixir. I hop to my feet. "Come in! Come in!" We greet each other with a joyous bear hug.

"I'm so glad you're here. How was your trip down?" she asks.

"Oh, you know. Lots of traffic. A few challenges getting camp set up, but no injuries to report."

She laughs. "Thank goodness for that. Now tell me about all your adventures since we last talked. Come on over to my place – you look like you could use a glass of wine. I've got hummus with garlic and sun-dried tomatoes and some smoked salmon."

"Oh my, Ruth! What can I bring?"

"Yourself, dear. Are you ready? Charli can hardly wait to see you again. We're in site 109 on the other side of the cactus gardens."

Chapter 27

After yesterday's drive, I told Ruth I'm ready for a hike today, but no crack-of-dawn start. Fortunately the forecast is for a relatively cool day by Tucson standards for early October, so we don't plan to leave until 10:30. I decide to familiarize myself with the layout of the campground, which is considerably larger than my last residence.

Strolling along the paved camp roads, each named for an animal, I see that many residents are already gone for the day, their trailers or motorhomes parked without any day-trip vehicles close by. I wave to an elderly couple sitting outside their unit, sipping from coffee mugs and reading. In the next lane, called Jackrabbit Road, I hum along with the lovely refrain of the old folk song "Greensleeves" drifting from someone's campsite. When I draw closer, I realize a woman is playing the music on an unusual instrument. I pause and watch her tapping strings with a pair of delicate mallets.

"Oh, I'm sorry," she says, looking up and stopping. "Am I disturbing you?"

"Not at all. It's lovely. What is that instrument?"

She smiles and resumes her playing. "It's a hammered dulcimer. I find it very relaxing to play."

"It's relaxing to listen to, as well."

I enjoy the music for several minutes before resuming my tour.

Shortly, I pass by a small group seated around a table, playing cards. Two women stand close by, observing the game. One of the players announces, "Read 'em and weep." Moans and a jumble of overlapping comments from the others rises and then fades.

As I stroll on past, a gravelly voice tells the group, "Man, I needed that damn deuce like a Chihuahua needs a curling iron!"

I freeze. Where did he come up with that line? Does he know Franklin?

Spinning around, I walk slowly toward the players, searching for a familiar face. One of the standing women steps away from the card table and I can now see a very elderly, totally bald and terribly emaciated man studying his newly-dealt cards. He raises his free hand and pulls on his ear lobe, nodding slowly.

It can't be. I'd know that gesture anywhere.

"Franklin?" I try to say, but all that comes out is a choking sound. I try again. "Franklin? Is that you?"

He raises his sunken eyes and focuses directly at me, his expression hard to read in his skeletal face. The player to his left looks back and forth between us. "Clay? Do you know this lady?" he asks.

Clay? That *is* Franklin's middle name, but ... am I mistaken? Grasping at straws?

"Ellie," he rasps. "What are you doing here?"

I can hardly breathe. What has happened to my husband? What's become of his mane of white hair? My God, he looks like he's lost 100 pounds – his arms are like twigs.

"What am *I* doing here?" I finally manage, standing only an arm's length away. "What ... what ... ?" I can't even begin to sort through all the questions bombarding my brain.

"Uh, fellas?" Franklin says to the group, "I think I need to call it a day."

The players and spectators immediately gather up the cards and coffee mugs, fold up their chairs, and move off. "Clay, you need a hand getting back inside, buddy?" one man asks.

Franklin shakes his head. "No, we'll manage. Thanks, everyone. Maybe tomorrow."

I watch the group disperse, trying to gather my wits. When I turn back to face my husband, he nods toward the picnic table. "Do you want to sit?" he asks.

Still at a loss for words, I follow his suggestion.

"You look fantastic, Ellie. It took me a minute to recognize you." He slides a bony hand across his totally bald pate. "The hair is very flattering. And you've lost weight."

"So have you," I say. "And sorry, but you look awful. What happened to you?"

He looks away for a moment, then meets my gaze. "I won't beat around the bush. I'm dying, Ellie." I close my eyes and fight back the tears. "Cancer. It's spread pretty much everywhere."

Battling for control, I ask, "Did you know before you left?"

He nods.

"But you didn't say anything. You didn't tell me. Why?" I say, my anger starting to resurface. "Why wouldn't you tell your wife of nearly forty years that you had cancer? Why wouldn't you tell your brother?"

Again, he shakes his head. "I didn't want to put you through all of ... this. What was the point? Why make you suffer through watching me go downhill with no hope of recovery? Why turn your life into that of a nurse, 24/7?"

I lean forward, staring him in the face. "Do you realize how hard your goddamn *Disappearing Act* hit me? All the self-doubt, wondering what *I'd* done to push you away? The pain, the ... the despair, the anger? How could you think all *that* suffering would be better than sticking together and ..." My tears are flowing full-force and I'm choking on my own snot.

"There's a box of tissues inside," he whispers. I rise and step inside his baby-blue camper van. A row of boxes of soup broth sit beside a two-burner stove. I spot a large pill bottle, a plastic cup, and the box of Kleenex next to the bed. I snatch up two tissues immediately to blow my nose and dry my eyes, and bring the box outside with me.

Franklin reaches out and takes my hand. "I'm sorry, Ellie. I thought I was doing the right thing."

I yank my hand back. "The right thing? What ever happened to 'in sickness and in health' and 'till death do us part'?"

He sighs. "Look, I know you would have stuck by my side. There's no doubt in my mind. You would have driven me to chemo appointments and sat with me, cleaned up after me when I couldn't hold anything down. You would have tried to talk me into even more treatments when the first round failed, even though the doctors said there was virtually no chance anything would work. You would have helped me shave off the remaining patches of my hair when it started falling out in clumps. You would have concocted nutritious smoothies for me when I could no longer manage food that I had to chew." He reaches out for my hand again, and this time I let him take it.

"But why put you through all that, Ellie? I thought I'd be dead months ago, and now it's looking like I may be here for another month, two at the most. Bottom line – I'll be gone soon. This way, you got a jump start on getting through the grieving process and you didn't have to wade through all the mess to get there."

I pull my hand from his weak grasp again and take a step backwards. "No. That's not how it works. I've been going through a grieving process, but grieving for our failed marriage. And I'm not exactly at the end of *that* tunnel yet, not even after close to a year. Don't imagine that you've saved me any grief. You've hurt me! You made this incredibly important, life-changing decision all on your own, without consulting me! How could you have so little faith in our relationship?"

"Ellie, I …"

"You stole a year of our lives. We'll never have it back!"

"Please, Ellie. Just listen. I …"

I shake my head, backing away further. "No, I can't talk about this anymore right now. I've got to think. I just … can't."

Before I can escape, he calls out, "Wait, Ellie. I need help."

"You should have thought of that before you walked out on me."

"I mean," he stutters, "I literally need help getting back in bed." I gape at him, realizing he may actually be too weak to make it on his own. "I'm sorry," he whispers.

My heart breaks. I don't know if I've ever been so angry at someone, but there's a part of me that still loves him. "Why in the world are you not staying somewhere where there are people to take care of you?" I ask, helping him to stand. It's like lifting a wounded robin – he weighs next to nothing.

"I have a room in a hospice facility waiting for me," he says once I've got him lying in bed and he's had a chance to catch his breath. "I wanted to stay here as long as I could, but I'm starting to rely too much on the kindness of strangers."

"Who are you – Blanche DuBois?" I say, trying to smile. *A Streetcar Named Desire* was one of our favorite movies – we've probably watched it together a dozen times, and I know its most famous line quite well.

"Nah, I'm much prettier," he whispers through his chapped lips before closing his eyes. Within moments, he's asleep.

Chapter 28

"Oh, there you are! I was getting worried about you." Ruth waves when she spots me shuffling back to my site. I'd totally forgotten about meeting her to go for a hike. "Dear, what's wrong?" she says as I draw closer. I know my face must be a mess – puffy eyes, red nose. I've seen that version enough times in the mirror during this past year.

"He's here," I mutter and begin to cry again.

"Who's here?" she asks, holding wide her arms and pulling me into a hug.

"Franklin," I sob. "I found him. And he's dying."

I cling to her like she's the life vest that might save me from drowning. "Come on, dear. Let's go to my trailer." She leads me by the hand as I stumble along, blinded by my tears. Settling me in a chair, she puts on water for tea.

"Now, tell me what's happened."

I dry my face and blow my already-tender nose. Charli plants herself on my lap, staring up into my eyes with an expression that I can only interpret as concern. She reaches up with a front paw and touches my cheek softly, claws withdrawn into her tiny foot. "She wants to take care of you," Ruth says, and I give the cat a reassuring pat. Not that I'm the least bit okay.

"My husband is camped here. And he's dying of cancer. He looks terrible – like a skeleton." I stare at the cup of tea Ruth has set in front of me.

Ruth looks bewildered. "Surely there can't be two men in this campground who ..." She takes a sip of her tea, her forehead crinkled in confusion. "Is he living out of an old, blue camper van over on Coyote Way?"

I nod.

"But everyone calls him Clay."

I nod again. "Franklin Clay Dwyer. I guess that's another way he tried to keep anyone from finding him." Feeling my anger and frustration start to rise, I stand, dumping the cat off my lap and bumping the table so my untouched tea sloshes over the edge of the cup. "I'm sorry, Ruth. I really just need to be alone for a while. Go on your hike." I stride to the door. "I can't ..."

Tears pool in her eyes. "That's all right, dear. You do what you need to do, but don't hesitate to come back if you need to talk later. Or if you just need someone to hold your hand."

I nod quickly and hurry outside. Head down, eyes on the ground, I rush to my camp, hoping nobody will speak to me. Once inside, I pace, but it's ridiculous. Two steps one way and two back are all my tiny quarters will allow. How much room do I have here – 75 square feet? How I used to pace in my apartment when I was angry! I could get up a pretty good head of steam in a two-bedroom unit with a living room and dining area.

Snatching up the information packet they gave me when I checked in, I scan the regional map. Desert Haven Getaway is on the outskirts of Tucson and I spot a road that heads into the hills but isn't named on this map. I gather up a bottle of water and a roll of paper towels, since I only have a small packet of tissues, and hop into my car. Within ten minutes, I've located the unnamed road. As I had hoped, there's almost no other traffic around, so I pull off the pavement and set out on foot, water in one hand and a folded mass of paper towels stuffed into the waist of my pants.

I rant and scream, a raging stream of consciousness being delivered to an audience of cactus and rock, lizards and tarantulas. The pavement ends and I continue my march on gravel and dirt, my feet kicking up dust until I'm choking. My anger fizzles and I'm left with grief, sobbing into wads of towels, my legs now frozen in place.

It's almost like starting the entire horrible year over again from scratch. Except now I understand that none of this is my fault. Now I know my idiotic, bone-headed, selfish, short-sighted, irresponsible husband is dying.

I sink to the ground and lie on my back, staring up at the sky.

My sweet, funny, warm, generous, loving husband is dying.

I lie still, listening to my own breathing, my mind settled into silence. A few fluffy clouds drift overhead, morphing in super slow motion from a raven to a cat, a smiling face to a skull. I remember sitting with Franklin on our back deck, waiting for the sunset. We knew the colors would be more spectacular if there were clouds, and we passed the time before the sun dipped below the horizon to point out the shapes to each other, like a couple of kids.

And then he'd start. "Look, Ellie. That one looks like an elephant playing a ukulele. Don't you see it?"

Or, "See that one? It's a bowling ball wearing a tutu. Listen – I think it's dancing to Led Zeppelin."

He could always make me laugh. And now he's dying.

With considerable effort, I manage to roll onto my side and work myself back into a standing position. My limbs feel heavy and limp, like I've been carrying great loads and hiking immense distances. Concentrating on lifting my feet so I don't kick up so much dust, I stagger back toward my car. A pickup truck approaches – the first vehicle I've seen since leaving the pavement – and I force a pleasant expression on my face and wiggle my fingers in a little wave, praying they won't stop to ask if I'm all right. The truck slows, but keeps on going.

Back in my Jeep, I feel exhausted. I drive to my campsite and quickly head inside my A-frame. I gather up a change of clothes and traipse to the bathrooms. After a long shower to wash away the dust, I return to my camp, but pause when I see a note taped to my door. I snatch it and take it inside.

The script is shaky, but I still recognize Franklin's handwriting.

> Ellie,
> Please come talk to me.
> Love,
> F

I stare at the note for several minutes. What is there to say? I've never screamed at him before like I did this morning, not even during our worst arguments. Since I've been mulling over every disagreement I could recall over the past several decades, I recognize that our spats have been relatively mild, as compared to the stories I've heard from friends over the years. I'm afraid I'll have another melt-down if I go talk to him now. That's not how I want either of us to remember our lives together.

I'm not ready to talk to him. It still hurts too much.

When I start craving enormous quantities of cookies or cake, I force myself to set up a chair outside in the shade of my trailer to read. Which is a joke, of course, since I keep finding myself staring into space instead of looking at my book, but at least I'm not holed up in my bed, like I did too many times in the early weeks after Franklin disappeared.

I'm startled when Charli springs into my lap – I hadn't noticed her approach. "Hi, little one. What are you doing out of your house?" I say as she stares into my face.

"She has a knack for knowing when someone needs a little loving."

I look up as Ruth strolls closer. "Would you like some company, or should we come back another time?"

Replacing my bookmark in the exact spot it was when I first sat down, I set the book aside. "Company would be good. But I don't have another chair."

"There are a couple of shady canopies in the cactus garden with cushioned seating. The landscaping is quite pretty."

"Sold," I say, setting the book on my chair. "Can we avoid Coyote Way?"

"Absolutely."

***

I sit in the shade, staring at an expansive prickly pear cactus with red knobs growing at the ends of the outermost, broad, flat "paddles." The red pieces look like a cross between ripe strawberries and rose buds. Charli balances on her hind legs and stretches upright to sniff at the plant, carefully avoiding the numerous long thorns.

"So much for good luck coming in threes," I mutter.

Ruth doesn't speak for a beat or two. Then, "I suppose it depends on what you define as good luck.'"

I glare at her in astonishment. "Are you saying it was good luck to run across my husband when I'm finally starting to get my act together? Just in time to watch him die?!" I grasp the arm of the chair tightly, trying to remember that my anger is toward Franklin, not Ruth.

She doesn't answer and we both focus our attention on watching the cat delicately exploring the desert garden. Several minutes pass.

"I can't imagine how this could be considered good luck," I say, calmer now. If she has a theory, I'd truly like to hear it.

She reaches over and squeezes my hand. "Have you ever heard the folk story, 'Good luck? Bad luck? Who knows?'"

"Can't say that I have."

"I don't remember where I first heard it. Maybe in a yoga class. Anyway," Ruth says, gazing upward and biting her lip in concentration, "let me see if I can remember how it goes."

After a pause, she begins. "Once there was a Chinese farmer and his son. They ploughed, and sowed, and harvested their fields using a horse. But one morning, just before they needed the horse to plow the fields, the horse breaks through the fence and runs away.

"Well, their neighbors hear what happened and tell the farmer, 'How will you plant your crop? This is bad luck!' But the farmer simply says, 'Bad luck? Good luck? Who knows?'

"A few days later, the horse returns, followed by two wild horses. Now the neighbors tell the farmer, 'Now you can tend your field even faster, or expand your crop. What good news!' And the farmer says, 'Good luck? Bad luck? Who knows?'

"Then the son begins working with the wild horses, trying to tame them so they can work the fields. He is thrown from one of the horses, and breaks his leg, so now he can't help his father at all. 'This is bad news,' the neighbors say. The farmer answers, 'Bad luck? good luck? Who knows?'"

Ruth is perched on the edge of her chair, really getting into the telling of the story. "Soon after that, the king's men come to the village, rounding up all able-bodied young men to serve as soldiers in a war with a nearby kingdom. When they see that the farmer's son has a broken leg, they pass him by. Again, the neighbors tell the farmer how fortunate he is to still have his son home, since all the other young men had been taken away. And the farmer says..."

We say it together – "Good luck? Bad luck? Who knows?"

I don't know if there's more to the story, but its point is obvious. "Okay, I get it. What seems like bad luck might lead to something good and vice versa. But help me out, because I'm at a loss, here. What good luck could possibly result from this mess?"

The cat comes and joins us in the shade, stretching out to her full length on the ground. Ruth reaches down and rubs her stomach. "Let me ask you this, dear. Are you ready to forgive him?"

I clench my teeth. "Not yet. Maybe over time. But then it'll be too late." I breathe deeply, determined to remain in control.

Nodding, she says, "There's a difference between forgiving someone and forgetting what they did that hurt you. I felt a lot of anger toward David after he died. The doctors had told him what he needed to do to regain his health, but he continued all the unhealthy behavior that led to his diabetes in the first place. I've always believed that he could have lived a much longer life if he'd only listened." She scans the area surrounding us. "He would have loved this place. We could have shared so many journeys."

"Oh, Ruth," I say, seeing a vulnerable side of her that she's never revealed to me before. I reach over and squeeze her arm.

She clears her throat. "I regret that I was a bit of a shrew in the months before David died. I tried not to harp on him about his diet and lack of exercise, but sometimes I just got so frustrated with him. I wish I hadn't been so angry with him while he was still alive."

"I'm sure he realized that you only wanted what was best for him – that you were acting that way out of love."

"Ah," Ruth says, raising her eyebrows. "Would you mind repeating that?"

"You wanted what was best for him," I say slowly, realizing what she's doing. "But Ruth, telling David to follow doctors' orders really was best for him. That's not like what Franklin did. Leaving me without any explanation, keeping his illness a secret, cutting off all contact – none of that was *best* for me."

"But did *he* believe he was doing what was best for you?"

"Maybe." As shocked as I was with his explanation, my gut tells me he wasn't lying. "I guess he did believe it. But—"

She holds up her hand, signaling me to stop. "You can still believe with all your heart that he made the wrong choices. But do you think *he* believed he was doing the right thing?"

I picture him, sitting at the table beside his camper van, looking as sick and weak as anyone I've ever seen. After the shock of recognition, despite my verbal attack, his sunken eyes were still the same blue-gray eyes I've spent so much time gazing into. Suddenly, I'm remembering a vacation to Carmel-by-the-Sea. We're sitting on the beach just staring into each other's faces, everything else fading into the background.

I still love my husband, even though I'm furious at him.

"He thought he was making it easier on me. What an absolute fool!" I say shaking my head.

Ruth remains silent, letting me mull things over. We focus on the sky, watching the transformation of blues into purple and pink, like watercolors washing across a canvas. With the sun below the horizon, a breeze picks up and I'm suddenly too cool.

"Would you like to come over for spaghetti?" I say, rising from my chair.

"Sure. I'll bring the salad."

We stroll back toward my place, Charli hitching a ride draped around Ruth's shoulders. "I'm not ready to talk to him yet," I say.

"Just don't wait too long," she answers as we reach the point where she'll be turning to go to her site.

"I know," I whisper. "I know."

Chapter 29

Ruth stopped by my camper early this morning, asking about my plans. It was obvious she hoped I'd say I was heading over to talk with Franklin, but instead I confessed that I needed to organize my thoughts before seeing him again.

"Would an outing help? I promise not to interrupt your thoughts with Chinese folk stories."

That actually makes me laugh – I still remember how. "All right. Do you have something in mind?"

Silly question. Ruth always has a smorgasbord of fun activities in mind.

"The Desert Museum," she says. "I've heard it's fabulous."

I can't imagine being able to focus on reading informational signs about cactus and sand. "You know, maybe I'll just run some errands."

"Nope. You're coming with me. From everything I've heard, I think you're in for a treat. "

It's far easier to give in than to argue, especially since I don't want to hang around camp where I might encounter Franklin or one of his buddies before I'm ready.

During the drive, I browse through a brochure and map of the museum and realize its name is misleading, although, within the nearly 100 acres, there appear to be a few small structures that contain museum displays. "Mountain lions? Bighorn sheep? This sounds more like a zoo than a museum."

Ruth nods, pulling into a left turn lane. "Did you see there's an aviary and aquarium?"

"'Cactus gardens, pollination gardens, riparian corridor'," I read from the brochure. "Ruth, this does sound fabulous."

We park in an enormous lot and buy our tickets. "There's a raptor demonstration in twenty minutes, ladies," the ticket seller tells us. She shows us on the map where to go. "If you don't stop for too many displays along the way, you should be able to get there in time."

I feel like a little kid, in awe of the massive eagle that flies directly over our heads to pluck an award from the extended arm of the handler giving the talk on raptors. We follow the circuitous trails to gape at bobcats and a porcupine, river otters and a roadrunner, all housed in natural-looking enclosures. Tall spines of ocotillos rise above a lush landscape of barrel cactus, the now-familiar prickly pears, chollas, and hundreds of other plants, but the majestic saguaros tower above them all.

Franklin would love this. I wonder if he visited here before he became so frail. Has he been terribly ill most of this past year, or was he able to enjoy his life at least part of that time?

We take a break around noon with lunch in the on-site restaurant. "What do you think?" Ruth asks. "Do you want to see more or head back?"

"We skipped some of the gardens and the aquarium when we came in. I'm up for those if you are."

By the time Ruth parks in her campsite, it's almost time for dinner. "My turn tonight," she says. "How about hamburgers?" and I walk back to my place to fetch a can of baked beans and a jar of dill pickles.

After eating, I excuse myself. I really shouldn't ignore Franklin's note any longer. We don't have to get into a whole, kick-in-the-gut discussion tonight, but I could stop by to be civil. Maybe he needs help getting settled in for the night. Or was that just an act to gain my sympathy? He managed to walk all this way over to my campsite to leave that note.

Okay. No more anger. Just drop by for a few minutes.

Focusing on my new mantra – *he thought he was doing the right thing* – I turn down Coyote Way and walk toward Franklin's van. All is dark and silent. I check my watch, confirming that it's really only ten past eight. Could he be off visiting someone, perhaps engaged in another card game?

A soft voice asks, "Looking for Clay?" The man walking toward me is one of the card players from yesterday.

I don't correct him on the name. Keeping my voice low, I say, "Yes. I wanted to check on him, see if he needs anything before he settles in for the night."

"Ah. Well, he went to bed about a half hour ago."

"Oh." I realize I had been hoping to help him again. But probably he doesn't even need help. He was getting along before I arrived, so why would I think he can't manage without me?

The man offers a hand. "I'm Marv, by the way."

"Ellie," I say, accepting his greeting.

"Yes, I know. Clay had me track down your site. Even gave me the note to leave you if I couldn't deliver his invitation in person."

Oh. I wonder how much Franklin told his pal Marv about our situation. "Well, if you talk to him in the morning, please let him know I stopped by. Do you know what time he usually gets up?" He's always been an early bird, but maybe that's changed with his illness.

"Well, that varies. Really, he's up and down a lot throughout the day with naps." He lowers his voice further, stepping closer to practically whisper in my ear. "Frankly, he's getting noticeably weaker each day. His hospice nurse has been saying he needs to move into their facility or at least some sort of regular home. She says there's not enough space in his van to set up the equipment he's going to need to keep him comfortable. He was going to check in to the hospice facility yesterday."

"Why isn't he there, then?"

Marv just stares at me for a minute, not answering. His face is filled with pain, his eyes pooled with unshed tears. "Because he made a terrible mistake, and now he's afraid he won't have any opportunity to try to make up for it."

A lump forms in my throat. He's even closer to the end than I imagined. I was thinking we'd have a month or more to talk, to see if I can undergo a radical transformation – mutate into a shiny chrysalis, emerge as a radiant butterfly. Instead, we may only have a few weeks – maybe less – to learn if somewhere buried inside us we can find any remnants of the Eleanor and Franklin who shared thirty-seven years, three months, and four days of marriage before he ran away.

"I'll check back in the morning," I say, hurrying away before I either cry or scream.

Chapter 30

After a terrible night of tossing and turning, I feel totally frazzled. My mind wouldn't shut up, revisiting that scene when my husband stood by the door to our apartment, suitcase and gym bag in hand, telling me he needed some space. Cast in a new light, I played the scene over and over, going back to the weeks leading up to that day and wondering how long he'd known his diagnosis. When did he go in for tests, what symptoms led to him seeking medical advice? And why the hell wasn't I part of every one of those steps?

Feeling drawn to having a heart-to-heart discussion with my husband yet emotionally unprepared to do so, I call upon Ruth to go with me. We can talk, but her presence may serve as a buffer, avoiding a total meltdown on my part.

"I'd like you to meet him," I tell her when she opens her camper door.

"Actually, dear, I've already met him, only that was before I had any idea he was related to you."

"Still – please come with me. I need you there."

Ruth purses her lips. "Are you sure that's a good idea?"

"I know what you're thinking. I just need to ease into having the 'big talk'," I say, gesturing with my fingers to draw quotation marks in the air. "Please come."

"All right," she says, looking around for the cat before closing up her trailer. "Charli, shall we go for a walk?" The cat bounds over to her side and rubs her leg enthusiastically.

"Are you sure Charli isn't really a dog in disguise?" I ask.

"Shh," Ruth says as she scoops up the animal and places her on a shoulder, "Charli might feel insulted."

We approach Franklin's campsite and I spot his bald head amongst the people sitting outside his van. We won't be his only visitors, and my reaction flips from relief to irritation and back again.

My husband looks up and our eyes meet. He winks and I smile despite myself.

"Folks," he says to his friends, "I'd like you to meet Ellie. And – it's Ruth, isn't it?"

"You have a good memory," Ruth says.

"When your livelihood is in sales and marketing, you've got to be good with names." He introduces the others – Marv, whom I've already met; and Stephanie and Don, who are wearing matching yellow t- shirts with the message 'Happy Camper' splashed across the fronts.

Charli, who had decided she wanted to travel under her own power once we got close to our destination, marches into the center of the circle of humans and plops down on the ground, where she starts bathing herself, beginning with a rather unmentionable area, her back leg sticking straight up into the air.

"That reminds me of a joke," Franklin says, "but it might not be suitable for mixed company." Directing his next comments to the cat, he mutters, "Show-off," much to everyone's amusement.

Marv stands and addresses the couple. "Hey, how about showing me your motorhome. I'm always on the lookout for a model to move up to." I nod at him in appreciation as the three depart. I wanted a trusted friend here with me, not a collection of strangers.

"Hi," I say.

"Hi, back."

"So," I say, feeling like a schoolgirl on a first date, "how are you doing? I mean, *really*."

"Really? Well, I'm here, and that's more than I expected a year ago when the oncologist sat me down to tell me I was, in layman's terms, *screwed*." He takes a sip of frothy liquid from a tall, plastic container, then sets it back on the table.

"He didn't really say that, did he?" Ruth asks, sounding appalled. She doesn't know my husband's sense of humor.

"No, but he might as well have. Do you know how hard it is to get a doctor to answer a question like *how long do I have*? Obviously, they aren't going to tell you, 'Right, Mate. You'll kick the bucket in seven months, twelve days, three hours, and forty-two minutes.' Anyway, after asking everyone who saw me, I figured out the docs thought I had about six to eight months. Here I am, eleven months later. So, back to your question, I'd say I've done well." He smiles, and I'm surprised by how large his teeth appear in his shrunken face.

I swallow and force out the next question. "What are the docs saying now?"

He shrugs. "The docs don't really have anything else for me, other than trying out different pain meds." He looks directly at me and I nod. "Ellie, I'm ready. I've been ready for quite a while. It's been a good life, hasn't it? I mean, except for my stupid idea to keep all this a secret from everyone."

I feel like crying and laughing at the same time. "Yeah, except for that part."

"Look around us," he says, his face lit up with delight as he throws out both arms as if inviting the world for a hug. "Isn't the color of the sky a miracle? It can be a thousand shades of blue and gray, pink and purple, orange and red. And the desert – did you ever think such an arid place could be this beautiful? Look at that gorgeous agave – you should see it in bloom. Think of all the amazing people we've met, and the wonder of connecting with someone and really getting to know them."

Although Franklin has always leaned toward a positive outlook on life, I've never seen him so radiantly happy. I think he really is ready. If only I were.

"You know what I miss?" he asks, not waiting for a reply. "Real food. Something I can actually *chew*."

"They've got you on a restricted diet?" Ruth asks, sounding puzzled.

"No, but my digestive system has gone on strike. I can't seem to manage anything that isn't already liquefied, and even my smoothies are becoming a challenge to keep down. What I wouldn't give for just one single bite of a tender, juicy steak."

"What if you just took a bite and held it in your mouth, then spit it out?" I suggest.

With a sheepish grin, he says, "Yeah, I tried that. It was a hamburger rather than a steak, but same idea. Trouble was, it just left me wanting it even more, so I decided it was too frustrating."

"What about a steak smoothie?" Ruth asks.

We all consider that for a moment, then groan. "Liquefied steak. That actually sounds pretty disgusting," she admits.

"Ah, but you know what I really, really, *really* am craving?" he says, a twinkle in his eye as he grins at me.

"Homemade lasagna," we say in chorus.

Ruth looks back and forth at the two of us, a smile creeping onto her face in reflection of ours. "I'm guessing there's a story behind this."

Just then, Marv walks up, carrying two folding camp chairs. "Ladies, I thought you might be able to use these. Just leave them here when you're done." Before we can talk him into joining us, he's gone again.

"So, what's with the 'homemade lasagna'?" Ruth prompts as she and I sit.

"Ah, well it all started with a dinner party we had planned," Franklin says. "I had recently gotten my first promotion to a very junior management position. I'm sure I had been reading some book on succeeding in business, and I decided we needed to invite my immediate boss, his boss, and their wives to dinner."

"Which made me pretty nervous," I add, "but I was determined to help make a great impression. I decided I'd serve my homemade lasagna ..."

Franklin jumps in, "Which is utterly delicious."

"But takes quite a bit of time. Anyway, the week leading up to our party was the week from hell for me. Just six days beforehand, I was laid off from my job as a writer in the company's PR department, so I was trying to put together a plan for free-lancing while also polishing up my resume. Then my dad had emergency gall bladder surgery, and Mom was falling apart about that."

"And you had PMS," Franklin adds. I pretend to slap his arm, afraid that I'd hurt him if I actually touched him, no matter how gently.

"Well, Ellie didn't go to the grocery store until the day of the dinner party —"

"— Because I wanted all the vegetables for the salad to be as fresh as possible. So, he's home vacuuming and dusting and putting the leaf in the table, and I get back from the store and he helps me unload the bags."

"And I'm pulling stuff out and wondering what in the hell's gotten into her. Cat food? We don't have a cat. Boxes of cereal with names like *Sugar-coated Oo-ey Goo-ey Chewies* and *Choco Loco Kiddos*."

"But no lasagna noodles, tomato puree, ricotta cheese. Even though I distinctly remember selecting all of those and putting them in my cart."

Ruth leans forward, holding her hands face up in front of her as a question. My husband nods at me to continue.

"All I can figure is that, somewhere along the way, I grabbed someone else's cart and never noticed. I managed to buy fresh veggies for the salad, but that was the last department I visited before checking out."

"And she never noticed that at least half her groceries rolling along the conveyer belt were things we'd never buy."

"I had a lot on my mind," I say, laughing.

"So you had to go back to the store," Ruth says.

Franklin shakes his head. "Actually, my wife had a bit of a meltdown at that point. I was going to offer to go back to the store for her, but I've seen how much work goes into making her lasagna. She was already frazzled with everything going on in her life, so I told her to just go lie down for a bit and I'd take care of dinner."

"And I'm thinking – Franklin's never cooked anything other than burgers or steaks on the grill. So I guess that's what we'll serve."

"But I'd already bragged to my boss about how incredible Ellie's lasagna is, so I did what any guy would do when backed into a corner. I called up a nearby Italian restaurant and ordered an entire pan of lasagna, garlic bread, and tiramisu for dessert."

"It all turned out okay, then," Ruth says.

I giggle. "Other than the fact that the lasagna from the restaurant was pretty awful, yes, it did."

"But so what if my bosses thought you were a lousy cook? I think I earned points from their wives for raving about how much I *loved* your homemade lasagna and how much I appreciated all the hard work that you put into the meal."

"Ever since, I never know when or where a box of lasagna noodles might show up. He's snuck them into my purse, under my computer keyboard, rubber-banded to the shampoo bottle in the shower ..."

"I made sure we were never out of lasagna noodles," he adds with a wink.

We've shared that story so many times, poking fun at each other, finishing each other's sentences. All of us are smiling and I look at my husband, he of the Disappearing Act, and I realize I don't want to spend our limited time together by hashing out all the *crap* from this past year. I want to rejoice in the good times and experience being together *now*.

His face contorts suddenly and he sucks in air before wrapping his arms across his middle and folding his face toward his knees. "Franklin?" I say, rushing to his side. "What can I do to help?" I touch his shoulder gently, not wanting to cause him even more pain. "What can I do?"

"Get me my medicine," he says through gritted teeth. "The bottle in the red pouch hanging above my bed."

I spring inside his van and snatch up the pouch. When I step back outside, Franklin is sitting up but still in obvious pain, Ruth at his side gently rubbing his shoulder. "Is this the right medicine?" I ask, pulling from the pouch a plastic bag containing a bottle and a medicine dropper, and he nods. He measures out a dosage and squirts it into his mouth, then takes a few sips of his smoothie. It seems like a struggle for him to swallow.

"I was a little early on that one, but I don't think anybody's worried about opioid addiction at this stage," he says, his eyes still clouded with pain. He sits back in his chair and closes them.

"Is there anything I can do?" I ask. He shakes his head and we all sit silently, waiting.

"Ah," he says after a minute, "I think it's passed. Maybe I didn't need the Oxy after all. That doesn't kick in this quickly."

I reach out and take his hand. He offers me a shaky smile in return. Then we realize that the cat wants in on the act. She's insinuated herself between our legs and is reaching up to tap Franklin gently on his knee, much like how she caressed my face the other day.

"Hello, you," he says, patting his lap to invite her to join him. Charli springs aboard and nudges her head against his chin.

"Well, that's a surprise," Ruth says. "She usually tolerates men, but I've never seen her show the slightest affection to a man she hasn't known for quite a while."

"She sounds just like a woman I once dated," he says, and I know he must be feeling better. Still, he looks drained.

"Do you need to lie down?" I ask.

He nods. "Sorry. I wish I had more stamina."

"Come on," I say, helping him to his feet, then aiding him in climbing into his van and onto the bed.

"I missed you, Ellie. I have no right to say that because of what I did, but it's true. I hope you can someday forgive me."

I bite my lip and nod. I don't want to lie to him. "I'm getting there. Give me just a little more time."

We stare at each other for a moment. "I'll try," he says.

I give his shoulder a squeeze and nod again before stepping away. "Door open or closed?" I ask.

"Closed."

Ruth and I return to our respective sites in silence. Charli refuses to follow, sitting outside the door of Franklin's van, like a watchdog – or in her case, a watchcat.

***

That afternoon, I swing by his campsite to see how he's doing. As his van comes into view, I'm relieved to see him sitting outside, chatting with a thin woman wearing an enormous purple floppy hat that Ruth would probably love. She laughs and strides toward the site across the way, waving as she leaves.

"Entertaining the neighbors, I see."

Franklin looks up at me with a grin. "I warned her not to wear that hat if it's windy, since she might be picked up and get blown all the way to Mexico."

"I think there was a sit-com in the 60s that used that idea."

"That's right – The Flying Nun with Sally Field. As you know, I have no qualms about stealing material for my jokes."

"You must be feeling better," I say, noting that he has a little color in his sunken cheeks. This does little to change my impression that he looks like death warmed over.

He nods. "You know, Ellie, I can't get over you buying a camper and exploring the country on your own."

I bristle at this, but tone down my reply. "You know I'd told you I was interested in an RV. Several times. You're the one who said you wouldn't ever buy something like that, remember? You thought we'd be happier just staying at motels and it wouldn't be worth the money."

"Hmm. I suppose I did say that. So, I changed my mind when my situation changed."

"Hmm," I echo back at him. Neither of us speaks for a few minutes and I consider cutting my visit short when he breaks the silence.

"Can I come see it?" he asks.

"It?"

"Your camper. I'd really like to see what you picked out."

I shrug. *Why not?* But, giving it another thought, I ask, "Can you walk that far?" He couldn't even drag himself into bed earlier and I can't see myself being able to haul him all that way without killing him.

"I have a wheelchair. It's folded up over on the far side of the van."

Pushing him along the paved campground roads feels like taking the Queen in a carriage to greet her subjects. Franklin waves at everyone we pass, his weak arms only allowing a slight gesture. They all wave back and some stop by for a moment to ask how he's doing or when he wants to play cards again. "Clay – thanks for that tip on my swing, buddy." "Hey, Clay – I watched that movie you recommended. It was outstanding, man."

When we finally reach my site, I can tell he's worn out.

"That's the cutest camper I think I've ever seen, Ellie," he says, his voice weaker than ever.

"This was too much for you, wasn't it. Should I take you back?" I ask as he struggles to push himself more upright in the chair.

"Do you have a place where I could lie down for a few minutes? Either that, or tie that strap around me so I don't fall out."

Alarmed, I grasp his upper arm and help him sit taller. "Sure, I've got a bed I can slide out in a matter of seconds. But can I get you up the steps? That's going to be the trick."

"Get the bed ready and let's give it a shot. I think we can do it."

I prepare the bed and return to help him stand up. Grasping him around the waist, I push and lift him from behind as he hoists himself up the two steps and inside my camper. Another step and a turn and he drops to a seated position on the mattress before I help lower his body the rest of the way and shift his legs into a comfortable position.

"I'll bet you thought I was just trying to get you into bed," he mutters. I shake my head, but can't quite suppress a grin.

"Get some rest. I'll be right outside."

He naps for half an hour, then calls out for me to help him back to his own place. "Thanks for the tour, Ellie. You've got a great little camper."

I keep rolling this time, even when it looks like people want to come over to chat for a moment, and we get back to his site in a fraction of the time it took in the other direction. Again, at his request I help him into his own bed, where he's already asleep the moment I step back outside. I slide the door closed and head home.

Chapter 31

There's no one around when I check Franklin's site at 9:15 the next morning, and his van is closed up. No change when I stop by again at 10:00. It worries me that he's sleeping so late. He's always been an early bird, getting by on six or seven hours, while I've been the one who could sleep in. Even when he was sick, he would be up by 7:00 A.M.

I return to my place, determined to complete at least *one* chapter of proofreading today, but again I find myself staring at the same paragraph for minutes at a time, my mind refusing to focus. I back up and force myself to read the first sentence out loud.

> Josephine felt she must return weather he would welcome her or not.

I moan. I must have read that sentence a dozen times, but still missed the author's use of *weather* when he should have used *whether*. Marking the error, I scan the sentence again and realize that the character's name was given as *Josephina* in earlier references. I save my work, realizing I can't trust anything I've looked at this morning, and shut down my laptop.

If Franklin's van is still closed up, I'm going to knock. What if he isn't just sleeping? What if he's gotten worse but doesn't have the strength to call for help? I speed-walk to Coyote Way, breaking into a trot when I don't see any signs of life outside his van.

"Franklin?" I say, knocking on the sliding door and holding my ear close to the vehicle so I might hear any sounds from inside. "Are you awake?" I say louder. I press my ear to the door, but hear nothing.

Grasping the door handle, I give it a yank, but it doesn't budge. I try the other doors – locked. His wheelchair is folded and leaning against the driver's side of the van, right where I left it yesterday. "Franklin!" I shout, now pounding on the side of the van. "Are you all right?" *Oh my God – could he have died?* "Franklin!"

I spin around, hoping by some miracle to spot one of his pals to come help me break in. Isn't that something guys know how to do – slip some do-dad along a window to trip the lock? Or maybe someone has a hammer and we can break out a window to get in. *Where is everyone?* Realizing the people in the front office must have tools, I scurry over there and fling open the door.

"Help me!" I gasp, my heart pounding so hard I think it's trying to escape my chest. "My husband is locked in his van! He's dying!"

The woman behind the counter leaps to her feet. "What site are you in?" she says, a phone in her hand. "I'm calling 9-1-1."

Why does she want my site number? "I'm in ... um ..." I can't think straight. Oh – she needs to know where Franklin is camped so the emergency people know where to go.

"I don't remember, but I need someone who can get inside *now*. Do you have a hammer?"

She holds up her hand, turning slightly away from me to focus on her call. "One of our guests is reporting that her husband is locked inside their vehicle and is having a medical emergency."

"I need a hammer!" I scream. When she holds her index finger in the air – *just a minute* – I turn away and dash through the camping supply store, searching for something I can use. Grabbing a large wrench from its display spot, I run out the door and head back to Franklin's camp, ignoring the woman shouting for me to wait.

All this running is more than my body can handle. I'm forced to slow down before I collapse, but I stumble forward as fast as I am able, gasping for air and clutching my side with one hand.

A voice calls out. "Ellie, stop! It's okay. He's not here."

It's his pal, Marv. I press a hand to my chest, feeling my heart pounding. "Oh, thank God. I thought ..." I do my best to sound less frantic, although he's clearly aware that I was in full panic mode.

"Are you all right?" he asks as he catches up with me.

I nod, still catching my breath. "Where is he?" I manage, feeling like a dolt. As if Franklin now needs my permission to go anywhere. "Is he visiting friends? I'll just come back later," I say, trying to sound casual.

"No. He called me very early this morning. He was having one of his, uh, *pain episodes*, and he couldn't keep anything down, not even his meds. I contacted hospice, and we moved him into a room at their facility. I'm sorry I hadn't come by to tell you yet, but I just got back."

Marv looks exhausted. That should have been me. Instead, I was sleeping until a comfortable hour, eating breakfast, attempting to proofread some stranger's stupid manuscript. I'm angry at Franklin for the year we've lost and angry at myself for not somehow *knowing* he needed help during the night. Shouldn't I have known?

"I need to see him. Is he able to ... I mean, are they saying how much time ..." I'm having trouble swallowing.

Marv places a hand on my shoulder. "Once they got him hooked up to the IV, he seemed to be doing a lot better. He's got one of those buttons to push to deliver morphine when he needs it. I know he would really appreciate it if you went to see him."

I nod, biting my lip.

"And no, they wouldn't answer my questions about how much time he has." He reaches into his pocket and retrieves a card. "Here's the address for CaringJourney Hospice. Do you think you're okay to drive? I could take you if you need me to."

I blink at the card, trying to get my eyes to focus. "Thanks for the offer, Marv, but you've done so much already. I'm sure I can get there okay."

The wail of a siren catches my attention. "Oh, dear," I say, and head back toward the office, walking swiftly. Thankfully, I spot an RV employee driving up and down the lanes in a cart and I'm able to flag him down.

"Are you the lady who reported the emergency?" he asks, skidding to a stop in front of me.

I nod. "False alarm. I didn't know that a friend already took him in for medical care. I'm really sorry."

He frowns at me before picking up a hand-held radio attached to the dash. "Oliver, here. You can send them back. No emergency."

She confirms and signs off.

"So, lady, were you coming back to pay for that tool you took?"

"Oh. Sorry! No, actually I don't need it after all. Now, where did I leave it?" I say staring back along the way I just came. "It's got to be along here somewhere."

He sighs and closes his eyes for a moment. "Hop on. We'll look for it together."

Sheepishly, I climb aboard and he drives slowly along the paths leading back toward Franklin's van. The wrench is lying on the ground right where Marv stopped me.

"Thanks for your help," I call out as Oliver drives away. "Sorry!"

I feel like a nitwit, but that's not important right now. Heading back to my vehicle, I text Ruth to let her know that my husband has been admitted to a hospice facility and that I'm on my way there.

Chapter 32

The exterior is attractive, a pale pink adobe-style building with a red ceramic tile roof over the entrance. Multiple wings spread away from the center, flowering bushes and leafy trees soften the lines of the structure. Inside, the reception area makes me think of a fine hotel. I'm relieved, remembering visiting my grandmother in a nursing home when I was just out of college. This seems nothing like that stark and dreary setting.

Walking down the hallway, however, I start to wonder if the entrance was just a façade. Hand rails line both walls, taking on much more of a hospital look. I hesitate at the entrance to the door for Suite 7, sitting slightly ajar. I rap and push my way inside.

Franklin is sitting in a cushy recliner opposite a hospital bed. Another chair, a couch, and coffee table sit close by, forming a cozy sitting area. Oversized windows let in abundant light, and there's even a glass door leading to an outdoor courtyard. The décor is southwestern, with the light brown bedspread matching the brown and teal upholstery of the patterned couch. One wall is painted in a matching teal. If not for the tell-tale shape of the bed, you'd think this was a deluxe hotel room.

"Ellie, I'm so glad to see you. I wasn't sure if you would come." He smiles and rearranges a blanket over his lap, although I find the room a bit too warm. A rolling stand beside him holds several IV bags of fluid and a tube runs down from those and disappears beneath the open collar of his shirt.

"Of course I came." I sit on the couch and study his face which I'm still having trouble reconciling with the many images I have in my memory of what he's supposed to look like.

"Not bad, huh?" he says, sweeping an arm to take in the attractive room and lovely view of the outdoor landscaping and distant mountains. "It's even prettier than I remembered from when I came for a tour."

"It's great," I say, but then burst into tears.

"Hey, hey," he says, beckoning me closer. I slide the other chair right next to his and sit. He takes my hand in both of his. "I forget that you haven't had a year to come to grips with all this. I know – that's my fault."

"Yeah," I manage, dabbing at my eyes, "It is."

"Yeah." He rubs my back in slow circles. Isn't this something – he's dying and *I'm* the one being comforted.

"I kind of freaked out when I couldn't rouse you at your van this morning."

"Oh, dear. I asked Marv to be sure to tell you…"

"No, it's not his fault. This was just before he got back." I describe my panic and demands for a hammer, but as I tell the story, it starts sounding more and more absurd to me. By the time I get to the part where I heard the sirens heading toward the campground, I've started laughing.

"Where's the emergency, ma'am?" I say, deepening my voice.

Speaking in a higher pitch, "We have no idea, but look for a purple-faced woman wielding a large wrench."

Franklin jumps in with a scratchy falsetto. "We think she's having a bad acid trip," he squeaks. "Either that, or her husband's *plumbing* needs adjustment." He wiggles his almost nonexistent eyebrows with the word *plumbing* and we're both laughing until tears roll down our cheeks.

"It wasn't *that* funny," he says once he regains enough composure to speak again.

In any other setting, he's probably right, but I've never felt such a need to laugh as I did just now.

"So, on a serious note," he says, "I've been worried about what happened to you when Hurricane Janelle came through. I assume the apartment wasn't habitable afterwards?"

"No, there was structural damage and water damage on top of that. But I knew when I evacuated that I wouldn't be going back."

"And your financial situation?"

I shrug, not sure if I want to tell him how much I've fretted over my money issues. If he hadn't taken off like he did, none of that would have been a problem.

"Hmm – not so good. That's what I was afraid of," he says. "I apologize for that. I really didn't expect to hang around nearly this long. You were supposed to get everything much sooner than this." He points across the room to the built-in dresser drawers. "There's a large, tan envelope in the bottom drawer. Can you bring it over?"

I retrieve the packet and pause, reading the return address.

Silver, Hollingsworth, Ellingwood, & Lippman, P.C.; 10254 Borden Pl., Tucson, Arizona.

That's definitely a law firm. Surely he isn't serving me with divorce papers at this late date.

It's quite the opposite. The envelope contains a detailed listing of his financial accounts; a copy of his will, plus a declaration dated nine months ago affirming that I am still his sole beneficiary; a summary page from his annuity, again showing me as the joint-and-survivor recipient of those funds upon his death; and a copy of the title to his van, with my name listed as co-owner.

Franklin points out the business card attached to the bundle. "Mike Lippman has all the originals on file, and I'd instructed him to track you down through Hank once I kick the bucket."

I grimace at the phrase.

"I hope I assumed correctly that you've been keeping in touch with my brother."

"I have. I went to him first when the storm was coming. You need to call him, Franklin. He's suffered with this disappearing act of yours too, you know." I set down the papers and walk over to the glass door, my head swimming. He abandoned me, but turned right around and made sure all his finances were in order to help me after he died. I feel queasy trying to navigate the emotional storm between my anger and my grief.

I do acknowledge this – the lunkhead honestly believed he was doing right by me.

"I'll call him today."

We're both silent for several minutes. "Ellie, I'd like to sit outside for a while. Can you help me with Rover, here?" He indicates the IV pole and its "leash" coiling into the neck opening of his shirt.

As I help him stand, he has me handle the rolling IV stand while he grasps my shoulder for balance. "You sure you can walk that far?" I ask, eyeing the dozen or so steps to the nearest chair on the patio.

"With your assistance, yes."

We slowly make our way onto the patio and I get him settled down. It's even warmer outside than in, but he asks me to bring the blanket for his lap. As I step through the door again, he moans and grasps the arm of the chair, his knuckles white. It's an even more horrifying sound than when I heard him crying out in pain yesterday. With his other hand, he grabs a small tube-like device coming off a box attached to the IV pole and presses the red button on its end. I hear a beep.

"What can I do?" I ask, hurrying to kneel beside him. "Did you just call for a nurse?"

He shakes his head, his eyes clenched tight. "Morphine," he whispers, breathing rapidly. He groans and pushes the button several more times, but I don't hear anything.

All I can think to do is to place my hand on his shoulder. My god, if I tried to massage it, I swear his bones might snap in two.

His breathing slows and he shifts to sit up straight. "Okay," he rasps. "That's better. The morphine takes a minute and the damn machine won't let me have another dose right away."

"Why not?" I fume. "Are they afraid you might become addicted? You're in hospice, for Christ's sake. What difference would it make?"

He attempts a grin, but it's pretty ghastly. "I guess it's so I don't accidentally kill myself."

"That's not funny, Franklin."

A middle-aged, African American man steps out onto the patio, wearing whimsical scrubs with brilliant stars and galaxies floating against a deep purple background. His head is shaved, but it's a much more robust look on him than on my husband's bony head. "Hey, Mr. D," he says as he checks the fluid bags on Franklin's IV pole, "how is your pain level?"

"About 3 right now. I gave myself a dose of morphine several minutes ago." Turning to me, he adds, "Marcus, this is my wife, Ellie."

We shake hands and with a subtle move, he steps over to a dispenser mounted beside the door frame and squirts something onto his hands, rubbing them as he turns back. "Pleased to meet you, Ellie. I'm your husband's nurse during the day; I'm sure you'll meet Alejandra if you're here in the evening."

"I think I need to lie down." Franklin's voice is weak and it looks like he's fighting to keep his eyes open.

Marcus lifts my husband to his feet in a smooth motion, wraps an arm around him for support and steers the IV pole with his other hand. I try to feel useful by closing the door behind them as the nurse helps Franklin into bed. "All right, Mr. D. Your call button is right here and I've clipped your morphine button next to your other hand. You need anything else right now?"

He barely moves his head, but he's signaling "no." Moments later, his breathing deepens and the muscles in his face go slack. I hope that means his pain level has dropped to zero.

While he sleeps, I stroll around the grounds, discovering private little nooks where I can sit on a bench or chair and reflect on the lovely surroundings. Difficult as it is to accept that Franklin's life is winding down, I'm glad that we are going through this in such a calm and peaceful place.

Did I just use the word "we"? Does it feel like Franklin and I are a "we" again? Perhaps.

Am I ready to forgive him? As Ruth would surely say, "If not now, when?"

When I return to Franklin's room, he is propped up in bed, a tiny spoon in his hand, contemplating a plastic cup on the over-bed table in front of him. "I had a craving for chocolate," he says as he looks up and sees me. "So far, I've managed two bites of this pudding. I'm trying to decide if I dare go for three."

Before I can ask what he's concerned about, he drops the spoon and snatches up a kidney-shaped bowl and spits up into it. I hurry beside him and help steady the container as he dry heaves. "Shall I get you some water to rinse with?" I ask once he collapses onto his back. He nods, and I step into the bathroom where I find a dispenser of small paper cups. Filling one with tap water, I return to his side and help him raise it to his lips. He takes a miniscule sip, swishes it around in his mouth, then reaches for the basin again to spit it out.

"More water?" I ask, holding the cup.

"No," he whispers. "When I get like this, I can't even keep water down."

I roll the table away from his bed. "I wish you didn't have to go through all this."

He manages a weak smile. "It could be a lot worse."

"How's that?"

He reaches out to me and I come close so we can hold hands. "It would be a lot worse if you weren't here with me, my love. I'm sorry I was such an idiot. I hope you ..." He shakes his head. "No, that's not fair of me to ask," he mutters to himself.

I reach out and cup his cheek in my hand. "Life isn't fair. But I know one thing. I have loved you for forty years, and I still love you today. If you were asking if I could forgive you, my answer is yes."

Franklin clasps his bony hand over mine and we stare into each other's moist eyes. "How you can love an old fool like me is a complete mystery."

"You may be an old fool," I say, "but you're *my* old fool."

He drifts off to sleep again, just a hint of a smile on his lips. I figure out which buttons to push to lower the head of the bed, then lean over and kiss him on the cheek. "Sleep tight, sweetheart. I'll be back first thing in the morning."

Chapter 33

"You've got a couple of special visitors, Mr. D." Marcus swings open the door for Ruth to enter, carrying a two-toned plastic box by its handle. Vertical columns of openings line the upper half of the side I can see. Marcus closes the door to the hallway and Ruth sets the box down on the coffee table. I can see a little, pink nose poking into one of the open slats.

"You've brought my little buddy!" Franklin says, adjusting his bed so he can sit up higher.

"That's right, I'm here," Ruth says, "and Charli too, big buddy."

Everyone laughs. "I didn't mean to overlook you, Ruth. I'm happy to see you, too."

She waves off his apology with a grin. Opening the door to the carrier, Charli explodes out of her container like a Jack-in-the-box. She freezes, turning her head this way and that, checking out this new environment, her tail dancing slowly from side to side.

"She probably needs to explore everything before I bring her over to your bed," Ruth explains. But, just as she says that, Charli marches directly toward the bed, leaps up onto the foot of the mattress, and delicately tiptoes up onto Franklin's lap, her eyes focused on his face the entire time.

"We find that animals often have a sixth sense when they're interacting with our patients," Marcus says. "Even a high-energy pup might turn into the most mellow dog you've ever seen when its owner is here in a hospice setting."

Franklin, stroking the cat's back, says to her, "What's that you said, Charli? You say you have a sixth sense?" He continues in a high falsetto, "I can see dead people!"

"Oh, man," Marcus says, "I didn't realize how that came out. Sorry, Mr. D."

But Franklin is still chuckling. "We missed our calling as a comedy team. Thanks for the great opening, Marcus. And would you *please* stop calling me Mr. D? Call me Franklin, or Clay, or even Doofus. If my late father shows up here, you can call *him* Mr. D, okay?"

"You got it, Franklin," he says, walking toward the door. "I'll be back to check on you in about an hour. You folks – and Charli – have a good visit."

After the nurse leaves, Franklin shows signs that he's fighting to stay awake. We lower the back of his bed and I straighten his blankets. Charli looks him in the face from a distance of about an inch, says *mrrr*, and curls up beside his head, purring like a motor boat.

"Listen to her," Ruth says. "I didn't know she could turn up the volume like that."

Franklin's breathing deepens, the cat's loud purring apparently not a deterrent to his ability to fall sleep. "Let's sit out here," I say to Ruth, heading for the patio, "let him rest."

Once we're settled, she asks, "How are you holding up, dear?"

"Better than I expected," I say, drawing in the relaxing aroma of the blooming sage plants nearby, their lavender blossoms waving slightly in the gentle breeze. "I think they've upped his baseline medications to combat pain. That's the only part that really gets to me – when he has an episode where he's desperately trying to get enough morphine to tamp down his pain. But he only had that happen once yesterday, and so far not at all today." I breathe in deeply through my nose, relishing the fresh scents of the desert garden.

"Are you scared?"

I pause, recalling our conversation when I asked my husband this very same question yesterday evening. "Not any more," Franklin answered. "But back when they first told me I had Stage 4 cancer? I was terrified. The doc in South Carolina discouraged me from even trying chemo, saying it would only give me a few extra months at best and would likely make me feel like shit for almost as long. I moped around for a few weeks, hoping you wouldn't notice anything, then started calling every major cancer center in the country."

"I could tell you had something on your mind," I said. "You stopped meeting your friends to play golf and you hardly made a single joke. When you left, I thought I had done something to drive you away. Or that you were having a post-midlife crisis."

He reached for me and comforted me. "Again, I'm so sorry I put you through all that, my love."

"Am I scared?" I echo back to Ruth, bringing my thoughts back to the present. "No, I don't think so. I'm incredibly sad. I'd give anything to get back this past year to spend it with my husband, even though it would have been a difficult path to follow." I pause, considering my words.

"But then again, I'm a different person than I would have been if Franklin hadn't left. I wonder if that *old me* could have coped with all this. I think she would have fallen to pieces and Franklin would have had to try to hold her up while his own strength was failing."

"Interesting how you're referring to yourself in the third person."

"Huh. I didn't even realize I was doing that."

I rise from my chair and peek into the suite. Franklin is still asleep, the cat curled beside him.

"Remember when you told me that fable about good luck and bad luck?" I ask.

"Mm-hum."

"You were right. Reuniting with my husband again before he dies is the best luck I could hope for. We've never felt closer."

***

That evening, just after the sun goes down, Alejandra, Franklin's night nurse, helps me get him into a wheelchair so he can sit outside with me to watch the sky transform from cerulean blue to a velvety black. He's no longer strong enough to walk the short distance to the patio, even with both of us propping him up. "I'll check back with you in a little bit," she says. "You've got the call button if you need me."

We watch the striated layers of color morph into gray as pinpoints of lights emerge in the remarkably dark sky. "Remember that time we drove out to the boonies to watch the Leonid meteor shower?" he asks.

I shiver with the memory, although the night is still warm. Tucking his blanket around him, I say, "We had that stupid air mattress with a leak. By the time we decided to head back home, it was like lying on a tarp. I could feel every little rock."

"But at least we had enough blankets. And we had each other to keep warm."

I laugh. "You missed seeing most of the shooting stars. You can't see the sky when you're lying face down on top of me, you know."

"I saw plenty of shooting stars," he says, "even with my eyes closed." He does that raised eyebrow thing that he knows always makes me giggle.

"We've had a good life," I say as we hold hands and watch the stars emerge.

It isn't long before he's chilled, so I wheel him back inside and call for Alejandra to help me get him ready for bed. She brings a nightshirt and extracts him from his other clothing, and I see his bare ribs and chest for the first time in a year. Despite knowing how emaciated he is, this is even more sobering.

I don't want to go back to camp tonight. Once Franklin is settled in, I follow Alejandra into the hall.

"Of course you can stay. I'll have them bring some fresh linens – the couch folds out into a bed," she says. "Don't worry – people tell me it's actually quite comfortable."

Once I've got my bed prepared, I go to my husband's bedside and watch him sleep. It's a comfort to see the covers rise and fall with his breaths. When I look back at his face, I realize his eyes are open, watching me. With some effort, he rolls onto his side.

"Come snuggle with me, Ellie," he whispers.

I walk around the bed so I'm behind him and work out how to lower the safety rail. Kicking off my shoes, I ease onto the mattress and scoot my body forward so it matches the curve of his back, the bend of his knees. When I drape my arm over him, he clasps my hand and holds my arm close to his chest. A year ago, the two of us could never have fit into a bed this narrow, but he takes up almost no room at all, and I've definitely trimmed down.

"This is even better than sleeping with Charli," he says.

"I would hope so," I reply, softly kissing the back of his bare head. Within minutes, his breathing tells me he's asleep again. A few warm tears leak from my eyes, dampening the pillow. After a while, I slip away, raise the safety rail as quietly as I can, and retreat to my own bed.

Chapter 34

Somewhere, I read that cats sleep between fifteen and twenty hours per day. Over the past week, my husband has drifted into a similar pattern of rest. Ruth brought Charli two more times, and the cat has insisted on snuggling close to Franklin's head throughout both visits, complaining vocally when Ruth picked her up to take her back to camp.

Hank arrived two days ago. I made him promise not to read his brother the riot act, but I'm sure he wouldn't have chewed him out once he saw Franklin in the flesh. Flesh and bones, that is. I gave them their privacy and Hank was red-eyed when he came out to the courtyard to join me. He comes and sits with me for a few hours daily. Cheryl will fly out for the memorial, once the time comes. Not surprisingly, Franklin already made all the arrangements for donating his body to a nearby medical center.

Marcus tells me it's only a matter of days. "How are you holding up?" he asks as we stand by the bed, watching the slight rise and fall of Franklin's chest. It's a question I hear daily.

My husband seems genuinely at peace with dying and his calm acceptance and child-like delight in the world he can observe from this room have rubbed off on me. "Oddly enough," I say, "it isn't as hard as I thought it would be."

Franklin whispers something. "What did you say, sweetheart?" I ask, leaning close to his lips.

The corners of his mouth turn up as he repeats his words. "That's what she said."

For a second I'm confused, but then I recall my exact words just before he commented. I laugh, tears of gratification pooling in my eyes. "I'm glad you still have your sense of humor," I say, stroking his head. He smiles weakly, his eyes remaining closed.

"Always leave 'em laughing," he murmurs.

He sleeps most of the day and evening, waking only to ask to hold my hand or to snuggle again. As I have all week, I spend the night in his room, waking when the night nurse comes in to check on him. But I'm sure I would have been up frequently even without her visits.

***

This morning I've dragged the reclining chair closer to the bed so I can be right in Franklin's line of vision next time he awakens. His eyes have fluttered a few times, but so far I haven't seen him actually open his eyes. It's quite early – the sun hasn't risen yet, although the sky is beginning to lighten and the stars above the eastern horizon have faded from view.

"Sweetheart," I say, "I'm right here. I'm going to be all right. You know I forgive you and I love you with all my heart."

I rise and lean over to kiss his cheek. "You don't have to hold on for my sake any longer. If you're ready, I am too."

I have no idea if he can hear me or feel my touch. His face is relaxed and the nurses tell me he is free of pain.

There is no obvious moment when he passes away. The rhythm of his breathing slows and slows again until the subtle rise of his chest simply doesn't return. I sit and focus on my own breathing for an unknown and immeasurable length of time, then press the call button.

Chapter 35

It feels strange to return to the campground for more than just a quick dash to grab a change of clothes. How my life has changed in just two weeks. How *I* have changed.

An insistent *meowing* outside my camper door tells me that Charli and Ruth have been watching for my return. When I open up, they both climb in and Ruth wraps me in her arms while the cat caresses me, weaving figure-eights around my ankles.

"Tell me what you need," Ruth says, releasing the hug but holding me at arm's length, studying my face.

"Once I figure that out, you'll be the first to know." I manage a tentative smile.

"Have you eaten?"

Although food was the farthest thing from my mind up until this moment, I now realize I'm famished. I haven't eaten since last night, and it's now late afternoon. "I could eat."

I'm escorted to her camper where she insists that I "sit tight!" while she buzzes around, pulling items from the fridge and pantry, rinsing and chopping, setting a plate overflowing with cut-up vegetables and a bowl of hummus in front of me – "This'll tide you over" – then turning back to chop some more.

"There're enough veggies here to feed everyone in the campground," I say, picking up a slice of red pepper and dipping it in the hummus. "I really don't think you need to cut up any more."

"This," she says, pointing with a large chef's knife at an onion on her cutting board, "is for dinner. When you called this morning, I was thinking of making meat loaf, but since that has to bake for so long and since I didn't know when you'd be back, I decided just to go with hamburgers instead. I hope that's okay."

"Of course! I really appreciate your taking care of me, Ruth."

"That's what friends do."

After the intensity of spending all that time at the hospice facility, I'm relieved to keep the conversation focused on light topics like Ruth's abundant camping stories and gossip about the goings on here in the campground while I've been gone.

"Last week, a couple moved in right next door, driving one of those rental RVs. You should have seen all the doo-dads they unpacked and piled up around their campsite – a large soft-sided cooler, two fancy camp chairs with little built-in tables and footrests, a gas "campfire" ring, a charcoal cooking grill, a lantern that turned out to be bright enough to perform surgery, a giant mesh tent to fit over the picnic table —"

"I haven't noticed many bugs this time of year."

"Exactly. But I suppose they weren't taking any chances. Anyway, that's only the specific items I remember. Watching them bring all that *stuff* out of the camper reminded me of the old fad in the 50s where they'd try to cram as many people as possible in a phone booth."

"I remember seeing pictures of that when I was a kid."

"Ah – a little before your time. So, when they turn in for the night, they leave all their *stuff* just sitting outside."

"Let me guess – the wind came up?" I say.

Shaking her head, Ruth continues. "Raccoons. I don't know if all the damage was done by one very ambitious critter or if her entire family joined in, but it wasn't pretty. They managed to unzip the cooler and then, apparently not pleased with the brand of beer they found, they also ripped open one side with their claws, exposing the insulating material. They knocked over the grill, spilling charcoal on the pretty outdoor rug and made off with the aluminum grate, which probably had food remnants all over it. They mangled the bug tent and the chairs, and pretty much messed up everything they had."

I dip into the carton of ice cream we're sharing for another spoonful. "That must have made a lot of noise. Did it wake you?"

"Mmm hmm," she says, letting a bite melt in her mouth. "And Charli was having a fit – I think she decided the raccoons were some sort of mutant cats. I didn't dare open the door to go outside in case she was crazy enough to try to take them on. So I just watched through the window as a raccoon that was easily twice Charli's size dragged that grate off into the desert."

"Did your neighbors come out to see what was happening?"

She grins. "I think they were too terrified. First thing the next morning, they stuffed 'most everything back inside their unit all willy-nilly, and took off, driving right over the remains of their cooler in their rush. A couple of young men sorted through the beer cans and liberated the ones that hadn't leaked."

Putting away the ice cream, I give Ruth a big hug. "Thanks for tonight and for making me laugh. I needed that."

"What do you think about a hike tomorrow?" she asks.

"That's probably just the ticket, so long as we're back by dinnertime. I'm meeting Hank to discuss plans for the memorial."

***

Even with an early morning start, the large parking lot for Sabino Canyon is nearly full when we arrive. Setting out for the trail Ruth has selected, we walk along a wide path along with numerous other hikers. Apparently reading my mind, Ruth comments, "Don't worry. The crowds will thin out once we break off toward the Phoneline trail."

I'm picturing a straight path following a series of telephone poles, strung phone cables arching overhead. When we turn and climb upward along a narrow, rocky path, I soon realize we'll be walking along a beautiful trail carved into the side of a mountain. The trail eventually flattens out, and far below us at the bottom of the canyon is a paved road hosting people on foot as well as the occasional shuttle vehicle. We are peering down on groupings of saguaros, yellow blooms of rabbit brush offering their splash of autumn color along the slopes. Our trail skirts around rock outcroppings and follows the sinuous curves of the mountainside. The views are stunning.

I'm not a religious person. I question the existence of both heaven and hell, believing that our souls – if that's what we choose to call the essence of a living person – do not continue forever after we die, nor did they exist forever before we were born. Yet, I can easily imagine the presence of my husband sharing the beauty of this place with me, seeing it through my eyes, feeling the roughness of the trail through my feet and legs, hearing the rapid *chur-chur-chur-chur* call of a cactus wren, which sounds like an engine that refuses to turn over.

Whether or not there's a heaven, my heart is filled with forty years' worth of shared lives, memories, and love, and that comforts me.

Ruth must sense that I don't feel like making conversation. We continue silently, pausing now and then to admire a particularly stunning cholla or to point out a flash of color as a tiny bluebird flits from a sycamore to a palo verde tree. In my mind, Franklin is standing right there with us, enjoying every bit of the experience. I'm sure this sensation will fade over time, but for now I treasure it.

Eventually we reach the top of the canyon and begin a descent on a steep, switchbacked trail. I tread carefully down the rough terrain, not wanting to turn an ankle. Ruth pulls ahead, her balance and sure-footedness belying her age, as always.

After a ten-minute wait, we hop aboard the open car of a park shuttle and nudge each other when the driver points out hikers far above us on the Phoneline trail. Our fellow passengers, many of whom have probably spent nearly their entire visit to Sabino Canyon right here on a shuttle bus, voice appreciative *oohs* and *aahs* when they spot the tiny figures who seem to be moving along a precarious ledge above an enormous cliff. "Only the most experienced mountain climbers attempt to follow the Phoneline trail," the driver declares over the PA system. Ruth and I giggle.

You hear that, Franklin? Now I'm among the most experienced of mountain climbers. Did you ever imagine such a thing?

Chapter 36

Close to thirty people have shown up for Franklin's Celebration of Life – or *Clay's*, since most of them met him here in camp and only knew him by his middle name. Hank was uncertain at first about holding a party rather than a somber funeral, but after he read his brother's note on the matter, he was on board. As per Franklin's wishes, we're holding the event here in the park-like area of the campground they call The Ramada.

Marv was kind enough to offer to kick things off as the first speaker to help set the mood. Ruth sits on one side of me in the huge circle of camp chairs; Hank and then Cheryl on my other side. Charli has planted herself off to the side of the shade structure, and is staring with unblinking green cat eyes at a low brick wall just behind the Ramada.

"I first met Franklin Clay Dwyer in early August at a campground near Munds Park, south of Flagstaff," Marv begins.

He was near Flagstaff? I didn't get there until after Labor Day, but we couldn't have been terribly far apart if he stayed there for a while. I'll have to ask Marv for more details.

"He was still getting around pretty well at that time, but it was easy to see that he was ill. Despite that, he was so friendly and so downright funny that in no time I felt like we'd been friends for years."

I glance at Ruth and she smiles at me, giving my hand a squeeze. How wonderful that my husband also formed a close friendship in a short span of time.

"He loved to get a card game going, but it had to have been because of the camaraderie. Because, God knows that Clay was one of the worst poker players this world has ever seen!" He waits for the laughter to die down. "I'll bet every one of you here today was the victim – er, that is the audience – of one of his jokes. He must have had a thousand of them. And his bizarre sayings – I know you've heard some of those. *You need that like a gorilla needs a can opener. He's as popular as an elephant in a movie theater.*"

The audience murmurs and whispers and someone calls out, "It's as crowded as an ostrich in a shower stall." Marv nods, grinning.

"I think what set Clay apart was that he was such a great listener. Now, lots of people can manage to shut up and give other people a chance to speak, but Clay really *heard* you. He was there one hundred percent, and he had a knack for knowing just what to say to help you get out your own story. Now, I'm not going to get into what *my* own story was, because we're not here today to talk about that. But I will say that having Clay as a friend to talk to and confide in was exactly what I needed at this point in my life."

I nod, thinking of how often I felt I had Franklin's absolute attention when I had something on my mind. He wouldn't offer advice unless I asked for it, helping to guide me to find my own answers.

Marv finishes up and invites Hank to speak. My brother-in-law stands and scans the audience. "It probably doesn't come as a surprise to any of you that my little brother was just as much a character when we were kids. Once you made the mistake of answering his 'knock, knock' with 'who's there?', you'd be hearing knock-knock jokes for hours. His favorite was ... Knock, knock."

The audience plays along. "Who's there?"

"A little old lady."

Smiling already since I know the punch line, I join in the chorus. "A little old lady who?"

"I didn't know you could yodel!" Hank responds, and the group moans. A few people try yodeling the words.

"I don't want to give the impression that my brother was simply a joker. He always had a kind heart as well. I remember back when he was about nine, he rode his bike over to a small shopping center close to our home. For the past week, we'd been seeing a man sitting by the parking lot entrance holding a sign that said, 'Hungry & broke. Anything helps.' So Franklin brought him a peanut butter and jelly sandwich.

"Unfortunately, the man told my brother to go away and take his 'damn sandwich' with him. Franklin came home in a funk and told our parents what had happened. They explained to him that some people begging on the streets are fakes, and his immediate reaction was to ask where he could find people who really needed help. Long story short, he started a food drive in his fourth grade class which spread to the entire elementary school and his class spent several hours helping stock shelves in the storage warehouse for a local food bank."

The crowd cheers and applauds. One guy in the back yodels again and we all laugh.

After Hank sits down, Marv says to the audience, "I'm going to tell one more story about Clay, then I'll shut up and we can tap that keg and open the wine for anyone who would like to partake."

More yodeling.

"So, Clay and I were driving through a small town on our way to go play a round of golf."

When he sees my puzzled expression – likely echoed by many others who can't picture Franklin having the energy to swing a club, much less climb in and out of a golf cart – he explains, "He was still getting around fairly well back then. He was thin, but not like he was by the time we both moved down here to Desert Haven. The plan was for him to play one or possibly two holes, then just ride in the cart, depending on how he felt.

"Anyway, there had been extremely high winds the night before, and we were seeing plenty of debris along the sidewalks and in the roads. While sitting at a stop light early in the morning on this mostly-deserted, small town main street, we saw a man walk over to a large limb that was lying across the walkway. He grabbed it, dragged it to the corner, then lugged it across the street. Then he dropped it right in front of the main entrance to a bank and walked away.

"I said to Clay, 'What do you suppose that was all about?' And he comes back with, 'Branch banking.'"

After the laughter and yodeling die down, Marv glances at me. Seeing my nod, he announces, "Let's party in memory of Franklin Clay Dwyer!" and people start heading toward the adult and other beverages, appetizers, and cookies.

As the party continues, a parade of folks stop by to introduce themselves and to offer condolences. I've overheard Marv asking people to keep things positive, so I'm relieved that nearly everyone stays away from comments like *at least he's not in pain anymore*. Instead, they mention his friendliness and warmth and, of course, his wacky sense of humor.

People gather in clusters. My circle includes Ruth, my in-laws, Marv, another of Franklin's card-playing friends named Howard and his wife, Sheila.

Marv takes another sip of beer and says, "Here's another Clay – I mean, Franklin story for you."

"That's okay, Marv. I don't mind if you call him Clay. That's how you knew him," I say.

He hoists his beer in acknowledgement. "Back at the campground near Munds Park, the owners used to put out iced tea and lemonade and an assortment of cookies late every afternoon. So, this one guy picks up a cookie, but then puts it back and reaches for a different kind. Glenda, one of the owners, spots him doing this and tells him, 'Don't put that back. If you touch it you have to eat it.'

"Without the slightest hesitation, Clay pops out with, 'That's what she said.' Well, there was total silence for a moment, but then everyone within earshot started roaring," Marv says. "Except for one person."

"Glenda didn't like the joke," Ruth says. My thought, exactly. Some women can't deal with even the slightest off-color comments.

"Nope. Glenda howled the loudest of all. It was the cookie guy who didn't laugh."

"He was embarrassed," I suggest.

Marv nods. "That's right. So, apparently Clay picked up on that because he made a point of introducing himself to the guy and inviting him to come sit with some of the people Clay already knew. He made him feel welcome at a point in that guy's life when he'd been going through some difficult times and wasn't feeling that great about himself." He clears his throat and contemplates his beer for a moment. "That was how Clay and I met. Over cookies. My divorce had just been finalized, and it was pretty brutal. My self-esteem was in the basement, but Clay embraced me like a brother and we became close friends almost overnight." He turns toward Hank. "No offense on the 'brother' thing."

"None taken. Any brother of Franklin's is a brother of mine, you know. Even if you can't decide what kind of cookie you want." The two men raise their beers in agreement and the rest of the circle follow suit.

"To friendship!" Hank says.

"To brotherhood!" Marv responds.

"To sisterhood!" Ruth adds.

I'm so glad that Franklin found a close friend just like I have. From everything I've heard today, he was surrounded by laughter and love during his final months. His health was failing, but for most of the past year he was still able to partake in activities he enjoyed, albeit in a limited way, take joy in the company of others, and, most importantly, know that he was adding happiness to the lives of people around him.

As the party winds down, I'm aware of the song playing over a set of speakers attached to somebody's iPhone. It is Garth Brooks singing "If Tomorrow Never Comes." Franklin and I loved that song, although many people would find it depressing, especially at a time like this. But my husband used to sing along when we'd hear it on the radio, and when Garth sang:

> If tomorrow never comes
> Will she know how much I loved her?
> Did I try in every way to show her every day
> That she's my only one?

he would always take me in his arms and whisper, "I love you more than words can ever say and you will forever be my only one."

I do know how much you loved me.

The crowd gradually disburses. I thank Marv for his wonderful stories and encourage Hank and Cheryl to return to their hotel to rest up for their flight home tomorrow. "I'm fine," I insist.

"Would you like to be alone for a bit?" Ruth asks – the only person still with me in the grassy area.

"No. If you don't mind, will you sit here with me for a while longer?"

"Of course," she says, and we drag our chairs under the Ramada shelter and sit.

"Charli," I say, noticing that the cat has returned to her spot and is again staring at something only she can see. "What are you looking at, little one?"

She rotates one ear in my direction, then steps forward and hops up onto the short brick wall just outside the shelter – the one she's been contemplating much of the afternoon. She meows several times, now staring intently at the brick beside her feet. With a soft *mrrr*, she curls into a tight ball and begins purring loudly enough that I can hear her from a dozen feet away.

"Cats see things people can't," Ruth says.

I look over at her, wide-eyed. "Okay, don't go all *Sixth Sense* on me," I say, moving to take a seat on the wall beside the cat and petting her gently. "If Franklin could have figured out a way to train Charli to act like she sees his ghost, he would have gotten such a kick out of that. One more joke for the road."

Epilogue

Happy birthday, dear Ruth, happy birthday to you!

Ruth sucks in a huge gulp of air and blows at the fiery mass of burning candles on the cake. When her first breath can't do the trick, her grandson, Gabe, and his partner, Ethan, lean in and help her blow out the rest.

"Does that mean my wish won't come true?" she asks her cheering audience.

"No way, Grams," Gabe says. "When you're ninety, you get to have helpers."

Carol, her oldest daughter, chimes in. "The only requirement is to put out all the candles before you set off the smoke alarm." Everyone laughs. Ruth scoops some of the whipped cream frosting from the edge of her cake and offers it to Charli, who licks it off her finger and promptly falls asleep again. She's probably close to ninety in cat years, but she seems to be aging well, like her human companion.

I look around the room at the smiling faces – Ruth's family. Although there are several I've not spent a lot of time with, I've shared some wonderful outings with Carol and Nick, who make a point of meeting up with Ruth at least once a year to visit a National Park or some other place with plenty of natural beauty and easy hiking trails. When Carol and I first met, it felt strange to realize that she is only five years younger than I am. Her mother – my best friend – doesn't seem like she could be old enough to have a child near my age.

Twice over the past ten years, Gabe and Ethan have scheduled week-long vacations to spend with Ruth and me. We've gone backpacking for three nights in Colorado, paddle-boarding in the Pacific Northwest, and snorkeling near San Diego. They call me Grandma Sorta, because Gabe says, as his Grandma Ruth's best friend, I'm *sorta* his honorary grandmother.

These people have become my family.

Ruth gave up driving four years ago and sold her camper. She splits her time between an RV community in Tucson during the winter and one near Durango in western Colorado for the summer. Both locations have options for renting a tiny home on their premises for those who don't have an RV or a tent. They remind me of retirement communities, with swimming pools and tennis courts, planned excursions to museums or winery tours, classes, clubs, potluck dinners, and shuttle services to shopping and medical appointments. She doesn't need a car.

I make a point of spending a month camped at each location while she's there. We still hike regularly when I visit – she can't walk as far nor as fast as she did when she was eighty, but we're not looking to set a speed record. With her trekking poles in hand to help steady her on rough terrain, it's not uncommon for her to pass hikers in their fifties or sixties, leaving them gaping after her in amazement. With the new t-shirt that I'm giving her for her birthday, I'm sure she'll turn even more heads – "*I'm* a Nonagenarian – What's *Your* Super Power?"

Arms wrap around me from behind and I feel the kiss planted on my neck. I hold Barry's arms with my own and lean back into him. "Hi, hon," I say, turning my head. "Did you finish your cake already?"

"Yeah, but I'm going back for seconds. Can I bring you another piece?"

"No thanks," I say, remembering an old TV ad where a woman buys pastries and attaches them directly to her hips. As I watch Barry stride over to the refreshment table, I admire his slim runner's body and muscular legs. Despite giving up running two years ago because his knees were starting to give him trouble, he still maintains his conditioning with hiking and cycling. It's not uncommon for him to take a long ride early in the morning before we head out for a hike, just so I can keep up with him. "Slow down, Marathon Man," I'll tell him. "Wait till you get to be my age." We often kid around about our three year age difference.

"You're beautiful and strong at any age," he'll reply.

Ruth was right, as usual. She kept telling me on the phone that she could hardly wait to introduce me to "a wonderful man who is just right for you." Barry is a snowbird from Michigan who's been coming to her Tucson RV community with his fancy 5th wheel camper for the past two winters. I flew up there to spend six weeks last summer traveling around some of the northern U.S. and parts of Manitoba and Ontario in his RV. Before I arrived, he had compiled a list of possible attractions and activities throughout the region that he thought I might enjoy. I was delighted when we discovered that we both also loved exploring pretty neighborhoods in the towns we visited, so we'd often end our days by strolling along a road, admiring the landscaping and homes along the way. He'd offer interesting observations of the residences, gleaned from his decades of experience as a Real Estate appraiser. In the evenings, we held our own little private book club, both reading the same novel and spending time discussing it once we finished.

Now Barry is just about convinced to sell his house in Marquette and go full time. Together.

Peals of laughter draw my attention to the sight of Charli perched on the cake table. Her pink nose has turned white with frosting. She peers around at her amused audience, then turns back to delicately help herself to another taste of the dessert.

"Allow me, Your Majesty," Barry says, carving a cat-sized helping of cake from her preferred piece and placing it onto a small plate. He gently relocates Charli to a spot on the floor beside her treat.

***

Thinking back on when I first met Ruth, I have to laugh at how clueless I was about living out of my camper. Now I'm like an old pro, the experienced lady who can help show a newbie that they need to flip a switch on the electrical box if they want their power to come on, or a trick to remember which way to turn their steering wheel if they want their trailer to move to the left as they back up.

Ruth and I still take one or two road trips per year, sometimes staying in undeveloped areas where we're camped far from another soul, just two old ladies who love listening to the gurgle of a brook or watching for shooting stars in the night sky. Other times we make plans to meet up with some of the numerous friends we've met over the years.

Whenever I experience a new place, I can still imagine Franklin there with me, his hand in mine as we admire a lovely view. Or I remember something funny he said when I needed a good laugh. Sometimes a spark of anger tries to ignite within me, but I've grown adept at sweeping it up and transforming it into a bright light of loving memories. I remind myself that I have the choice of immersing myself in negative flashbacks or setting them aside, knowing that I've already given them more attention than they deserve.

Barry is completely understanding and comfortable when I mention fond memories of my husband. He lost his wife to cancer as well, but that was only three years ago. She sounds like someone I would have enjoyed as a friend, and Barry has said the same about Franklin.

Today, we celebrate a remarkable woman's ninetieth birthday. She is my best friend, my closest confidant, my sister, my mother. I know she won't be around forever, but as long as either of us has any say in the matter, we'll keep finding joy in sharing great escapes together. And when she is gone, I'll strive to continue following the path she's shown me.

ABOUT THE AUTHOR

Diane Winger is a retired computer programmer who loves to seek outdoor adventures, either close by her western Colorado home or farther afield, using her Aliner camper-trailer as home base. She and her husband, Charlie, enjoy hiking, rock climbing, cross-country skiing, and kayaking, and fill their evenings with reading, writing, playing Scrabble, or planning their next trip.

She is an enthusiastic volunteer with the service organization, Altrusa International, with a particular fondness for their many literacy-enhancing projects.

Diane and Charlie are co-authors of several guidebooks on outdoor recreation. *Ellie Dwyer's Great Escape* is Diane's 8th novel.

http://WingerBooks.com

Dear Reader,

I hope you enjoyed *Ellie Dwyer's Great Escape*.

As an author, I thrive on feedback. You, the reader, are a major part of my inspiration to write, to explore my characters, and to try to bring them to life. So, please let me know what you liked or disliked. I'd love to hear from you. You can email me at **author@WingerBooks.com**, or visit me on the web at **WingerBooks.com**.

Just one more thing. I would consider it a great favor if you would post a review of *Ellie Dwyer's Great Escape*. Whether you loved it or hated it, or anything in between, I appreciate your feedback. Reviews can be difficult to come by. Every review can have an enormous impact on the success or failure of a book.

You can find all of my titles on my Author Page on Amazon – the link to it is **amazon.com/author/winger**. Please visit my page and, if you have time, leave a review. You can also "follow" me on Amazon to receive news when a new title is available.

Thank you so much for reading this book and for spending time with me.

Sincerely,
Diane Winger

Books by Diane Winger

Faces
Duplicity
Rockfall
Memories & Secrets
The Daughters' Baggage
The Abandoned Girl
No Direction Home
Ellie Dwyer's Great Escape
Ellie Dwyer's Big Mistake

Made in the USA
San Bernardino, CA
28 February 2020